Through
AND IN THE DARK

Through and in the Dark

So Much More Than Enough

DORIS SPEIGINER WHEELER

XULON PRESS

Xulon Press
2301 Lucien Way #415
Maitland, FL 32751
407.339.4217
www.xulonpress.com

© 2021 by Doris Speiginer Wheeler

All rights reserved solely by the author. The author guarantees all contents are original and do not infringe upon the legal rights of any other person or work. No part of this book may be reproduced in any form without the permission of the author. The views expressed in this book are not necessarily those of the publisher.

Unless otherwise indicated, Scripture quotations taken from the King James Version (KJV) – *public domain*.

Printed in the United States of America.

Paperback ISBN-13: 978-1-6628-1153-1
eBook ISBN-13: 978-1-6628-1154-8

TABLE OF CONTENTS

Introduction..............................vii
Dedication................................ix
Acknowledgement...........................xi

Chapter 1   Known by God 1
Chapter 2   Noted Trouble 24
Chapter 3   Appreciating God 37
Chapter 4   Keeping the Lord before Us 50
Chapter 5   Keep Seeking........................77
Chapter 6   Hope Filled Service.................95
Chapter 7   Hopeful Still 150
Chapter 8   So Much More Than Enough 161
Chapter 9   Called and Set Apart...............168
Chapter 10 Sudden Sorrow 181
Chapter 11 Ready and Set to Go 190
Chapter 12 A Blessed Conversation.............193
Chapter 13 Prepared for a Friend..............200
Chapter 14 Lesson Learned.....................217

Overview..................................221
About the Author 225

Introduction

The Author, in 1994 found self, and husband with new challenges, prompted by her husband's job (Design Specialist Engineer) being moved from California to Arizona.

Challenges involved finding a home, in a wholesome area. And a church of the SDA denomination. The Author, and her husband Bob, had in California. Grown comfortable with, for over 30 years.

The change of location and slower pace. Due to the Author, leaving her job behind, (Psychiatric Nurse, Behavior Specialist, and Group Home Consultant). Gave the Author, the opportunity, to explore her spiritual life purpose.

The Author, increased, in a diligent study of God's word. For her growth and her desire. To share, and inspire others. To live by knowing God, and God's word.

The Author, became active in, the ministry, of reconciliation.

Finding who the Lord God is. And what he does to fulfill his purpose was a blessing.

The Author, is, able to recognize her work in this world. Is blessed from her experience with God's, presence. Through and in the dark.

Dedication

To the gift of Salvation that was expressed, encouraged, and claimed, by faith to see fulfilled. Believed for their children's future. By my parents, and grandparents. To my seven sisters, myself, and all persons loved, and related to us.

Acknowledgement

Praise, glory, and honor to my awesome Lord God, Father, Son, and Holy Spirit, that daily provides counseling, comfort, peace, and rest as promised, and confirmed in the lives of family, and friends. Through, and in the dark.

Chapter 1

Known by God

On my constant attempt to become. Well acquainted, with the Lord God. I, find I, have gained great encouragement. In the priceless value. Of seeking spiritual growth.

My growth has come about, and matured. By me wanting to increase in knowing, and trusting the Lord God. I, learned the Lord knows me. And the Lord Knows the conditions. That surround me.

I, find to invest my time. In applying God's word. Just the experience of making the effort. Adds strength to my life. Because to the Lord God. I, am necessary, beneficial, and precious.

My Encouragement:

Christ Jesus, is my encouragement. By pursuing the way, I, see what the Lord Christ Jesus, lived, and taught. Is a daily challenge for my, growth. And I, am influenced. To seek the growth of others.

God's complete, knowledge of me. Gives me sound reason to seek his desire for me. I know all of God's desire for my soul. Is expressed in his word. God's word spoken is my deliverer. And it is my healer:

> "He sent **his word, and healed them**, and **delivered them** from their destructions. Psalm 107:20"

Acquainting myself with God's word. I, find is the way of God. By which I, am able by study. To acquaint myself with God. I increased in knowing the Father, the Son, and Holy Spirit. By knowing I, need them. in my life, as determined.

The Lord, prepares, and equips me by his word. For my destiny with him. It is the Lord God, that keeps me. As I, move with the light of hope. Through this dark world.

I, am led to abide in God's word. I trust the word is the way of victory. Because it is commanded by, the Lord Christ Jesus.

I focus on God's word for leading me to God:

> "That **thy way may be known** upon earth, thy saving health among all nations. Psalm 67:2"

I, know learning what the word, says about God (in three persons). Caused me to seek knowledge of God. And how God abides as one, in three persons.

The only way I, know the working of God, And with respect honor God. Is by hearing the word. And observing Christ's life. I, learn from the honor Christ, gives to his Father, and Holy Spirit. Christ Jesus' commands. All, to know, and follow his, word:

> "And this is life eternal, **that they might know thee the only true God, and Jesus Christ,** whom thou hast sent. John 17:3"

Reliance Upon The Word:

I have learned from gained knowledge. I, must rely upon the word of God. I, am led by the word, to whole heartedly rely upon God's word.

By the word of God, I find affirmation. To the merciful extent of how much I, am love. And how well I, am known, and cared for.

By the scriptures I, am being led. To seek Christ Jesus' leading me by scripture. The confirmations of the choices I am to make. Are clarified in God's word. And verified in the life of Christ.

I, find God's desire for me. Centers on his love for me. I, am motivated by knowing the Lord loves me. God by love leads me. And by love he restores my redeemed life. And allows my life, to testify of his love:

> "I am the good shepherd, and know my sheep, and **am known of mine** John 10:14".

> "But **grow in grace, and in the knowledge of our Lord** and Saviour Jesus Christ. To him be glory both now and for ever. Amen. 2 Peter 3:18"

Comfort From God's Purpose:

The word of God, by the provisions of the Holy Spirit, comforts me. I am assured of the Lord God, knowing me. By the Lord expressing love for me, in his word.

From the beginning God's purpose. Is expressed in his word. I find all of God's, written word. Is a comforting, and reliable. Expression of God's love. And it is for love's sake, through Christ. That God reveals his, soul saving purpose.

Desire for the soul of man to be blessed. Is revealed from the beginning. Love is made evident by God sending his Son. And God's provisions. to accomplish his purpose for mankind. Is confirmed by God sending his Son.

We have the word of God. Expressing to us God's purpose. The word of God has clearly established God's plans. In Christ Jesus, is God's salvation plans.

In love for us salvation with atonement by the righteous life of Christ. Was in place by Christ's position. That was purposed for mankind, before the world began:

> "Who **hath saved us, and called us with an holy calling,** not according to our works, but **according to his own purpose and grace, which was given us in Christ Jesus** before the world began, 2 Timothy 1:9"

> "According to the **eternal purpose** which he **purposed in Christ Jesus** our Lord: Ephesians 3:11"

> "According as he hath **chosen us in him** before the foundation of the world, **that we should be holy and without blame before him in love:** Ephesians 1:4"

I, have gratitude in realizing. The needs of mankind were fully covered. Before the world began. Christ Jesus our salvation had himself designed the plans that brought mankind salvation:

> "For **by him were all things created**, that are in heaven, and that are in earth, **visible and invisible**, whether they be thrones, or dominions, or principalities, or powers: **all things were created by him, and for him:** Colossians 1:16"

> "Then shall the King say unto them on his right hand, Come, ye blessed of my Father, **inherit the kingdom prepared for you from the foundation of the world:** Matthew 25:34"

The Lord Knowing Me:

The Lord makes it known to me. That he is the Lord over my soul. I, see what the Lord prepared for me. Was prepared because he knew the provisions. For soul restoration I, would need.

From The Lord's Knowledge:

It is from the Lord being well acquainted with me. That I know, it is in Christ Jesus that my Salvation is found. I, have in Christ Jesus, what my soul needs, to know, and to follow.

From God's word, I, learn that it is with perfect judgment. That the Lord God, my savior knows me. And the Lord, graciously supplies what it takes. For the way I need to go.

I, have found, it is even, a great asset. To know the Lord, disciplines me. To have what he, defines as quality life.

The Lord God, communicates by discipline. The reality of him knowing me and loving me.

It awes me to know with good purpose. The Lord, encourages me. I, have learned to be excited. Over the opportunity the Lord gives.

Even by oppositions aimed against me, I grow. I, have grown to know Christ better by beholding his life. Through the identified oppositions Christ faced, I, am instructed.

Taught by the Lord Christ's life, I, gain spiritual vision. Of the Lord God's glory, in the flesh. Christ in the flesh, is that which fully prepares me with hope.

I, have hope from the word of God. To live for the opportunity. to manifest the Lord God's glory. As I focus on Christ, I am delighted to recall. Christ lived for the glory of God his Father:

> "And the Lord passed by before him, and proclaimed, The Lord, The Lord God, **merciful and gracious, longsuffering, and abundant in goodness and truth**, Exodus 34:6"

The more I, know about the Lord God. I am purposed to increase my growth in the Lord. I daily seek to prepare for manifesting the Lord.

By increasing my knowledge of the Lord Jesus, and his ways. I, am with growing knowledge, prepared for service. I, am encouraged by how I, have recognized my need.

I have grown in seeing God, in Christ. The Lord has proven to me, that he is able, and faithful. In accomplishing all his soul delivering, and soul, restoring promises. To work faithfully in my life the Lord led me. To diligently search his word:

> "For whatsoever **things were written aforetime were written for our learning**, that we through patience and comfort of the scriptures might have hope. Romans 15:4"

Holy Spirit Speaks The Word:

The Lord speaks to me, by the Holy Spirit. That keeps teaching, and reminding me, of Christ's, words. I believe, and rejoice that the Lord, sees, hears, and responds to me, by his Holy Spirit.

Need For Maturity:

Due to the Holy Spirit, manifesting Christ in the word of God. The Lord Christ Jesus, is kept as my focus. I, am kept planted in God's purpose. By the Holy Spirit exalting the life, and commands of Christ Jesus, is the way I, mature.

For needed maturity in my relationship, with the Lord God. I rejoice that his Spirit, completely searches me out. The most blessed gift I believe I, have is truth. The truth of the Lord Christ Jesus, is by the Holy Spirit, living within me, and frees me.

Love Teaches:

I, am blessed by learning it is the Lord God, who loves, and teaches me. It comforts, and settles me, that God, teaches me, Christ, belongs to me.

I, have gained confidence in the Lord God's, preparation for me. To learn, and serve his way. I know as I, remain desiring. To be taught by the Lord. Faithfulness, in pursuing bible knowledge. Is required, for my, growth in maturity.

So much is being taught to me, daily. Because I, belong to the Lord Jesus. And the Lord Jesus, belongs to me. I am comforted by knowing the Christ Jesus, who is the Holy One, exists. And teaches me, by his Holy Spirit, for my soul's profit:

> "Thus saith the Lord, thy Redeemer, the Holy One of Israel; I am the Lord thy God which **teacheth thee to profit, which leadeth thee by the way** that thou shouldest go. Isaiah 48:17"

Place Of Relief:

I accept the value of the Lord God, abiding in, and with me. I know, and I, am so content. That I, am able to do all things, by God's, leading.

To know I, may freely go to the Lord, anytime. I, go to the Lord, with labors, and burden of myself, and for others. The Lord Christ, being the place I, go. Keeps me with peace, in my, soul.

I, know because the God loves me. He, is always there to guide, and correct me. I, have often experienced the Lord God's silent presence.

Being Blessed:

I, am relieved, and blessed to know. I, am kept, by the Lord. following me, with steadfast love. I, am blessed by the privilege the

Lord gives, for me to know the Lord. By what he, graciously shares, concerning who he, is for my good.

I, am blessed by knowing, the Lord regularly prompts me, to acknowledge him. I am blessed by looking to the Lord. In all my thoughts, and my, daily life activities. I, am blessed as I, seek to acknowledge him, in all my ways:

> "Blessed be the Lord, **who daily loadeth us with benefits**,
> even the God of our salvation. Selah. Psalms 68:19"

In the Lord God's knowledge, wisdom, and understanding, I survive, and stand protected, through and in the dark, of this world. The Lord God, has proven to me that his, integrity, for my soul, leads and protects me.

Over-rides Weaknesses:

I, have assurance that by loving, and knowing me. The Lord knows what it takes, to over-ride my weaknesses. The Lord God rescues me from me. Because it is his purpose, and his, pleasure, to see me grow, unto his, likeness.

The Lord, knows how, to magnify through me, his love. By the Lord God's understanding of me. I am encouraged.

It is the Lord's desire, for me to leave, all my weaknesses behind. That is why I, am led to seek him. I learned to desire things, that are in tune with what the Lord desires for me.

For me to allow my desire to please the Lord takes the Lord's help. Because of the Lord's help, I, am kept, in harmony with the Lord God. And that is my abiding desire.

Pleasure Found:

My pleasure is found in learning, claiming, and sharing the Lord God, and his promises. I, learned the promises given, by God, from the beginning, Were in love planned for fulfillment.

I, have learned all life-giving blessings, are to be fulfilled in, and for Christ Jesus. Just as God in his word promised, victory is in Christ.

I am encouraged by the Lord God's promise. That the Lord Christ shall never leave me. I have experienced that the Lord God keeps his every promise. In the loving merits and integrity of his Son, Christ Jesus.

Always Working:

I, have learned to recognize, and believe. The Lord God is always present, and working behind the scenes. The Lord is always seen by me, leading in the events of my life.

Recognizing the Lord God intervening. I, am led to know, the Lord God, never stops loving me. I, find the Lord is well able, and faithful. To give relief from burdens, and offer spiritual prosperity for my soul's growth.

I, find, I, can freely encourage others. Just by testifying of the Lord working in my life. And I am able to have good works that glorify the Father. By the Lord Christ being the true, and great light of my life.

Encouraged To Serve:

From my experiences with the Lord, I, encourage other folks. I, encourage others to know God is able, and faithful. I serve by showing I am benefiting from my growth in the Lord.

Growing to know the Lord more intently. The Lord Christ I, know he leads me by his word. The only way I, am able to serve, is by what I, receive from his word.

I, feel blessed to know, the Lord God does according to all his promises. I know what Christ the Lord, has lived for mankind, to follow, and is for me unchanging.

Christ leads the way to growth in truth. Truth I, learn is the essence of Christ my Lord. Christ being sent with mercy allows the blessing of grace.

I believe seeking Christ's righteous kingdom. By pursuing the righteousness life Christ lived. Promotes kingdom seeking, and is what leads to eternal life:

> "**Come unto me**, all ye that labour and are heavy laden, and I will give you rest. Take my yoke upon you, and **learn of me**; for I am meek and lowly in heart: and **ye shall find rest unto your souls**. For my yoke is easy, and my burden is light. Matthew 11:28-30"

> "I am the vine, ye are the branches: **He that abideth in me, and I in him, the same bringeth forth much fruit**: for without me ye can do nothing. John 15:5"

> "Wherefore **he is able also to save them to the uttermost that come unto God by him**, seeing he **ever liveth to make intercession** for them. Hebrews 7:25"

Christ is the light for my life that is ever shining. By his Holy Spirit, I, keep involvement ongoing, in his life guiding word.

I, recognize it is by Christ being the proven truth. That causes God's word of truth, to unfolding his truth tome. It is in God's word being true, that I, find life sustaining truth in Christ.

An Open Book:

I learned that even my thoughts. Are to the Lord God, as an open book. The Lord God's gift, of wisdom, knowledge, and unsearchable, understanding. Is found by hearing Christ's words, and observing Christ Jesus life.

I, am able to see my need to be instant in examining myself. The Lord God, even in his word discloses to me, what my thoughts are. By knowing the Lord knows my thoughts. I, am with gratitude, fearfully comforted, and encouraged:

> "For **the word of God is quick, and powerful**, and sharper than any twoedged sword, **piercing** even to the dividing asunder of soul and spirit, and of the joints and marrow, **and is a discerner of the thoughts and intents of the heart**. Hebrews 4:12"

Warnings Concerning Words:

Even before, I, speak from my thoughts. The Lord has in his word given warnings for me. From God's word I, receive admonition. Biding me not to act upon my thoughts.

I have been led by scripture to ask for forgiveness. Should my thoughts be of carnal prompting, or evil intent. It gives me relief to know my thoughts are known by the Lord God. Who I know loves, and leads me.

In love the Lord God, who has led me, to submit to him. I, can testify that the Lord has often redirected my choices. Often, and repeatedly.

> "If thou hast done foolishly in lifting up thyself, or **if thou hast thought evil, lay thine hand upon thy mouth.** Proverbs 30:32"

> "Repent therefore of this thy wickedness, and **pray God, if perhaps the thought of thine heart may be forgiven thee.** Acts 8:22"

Always For My Good:

I, know from personal life experience. The Lord God, is, always working for my good. I, often am led to acknowledge to myself. The Lord moment, by moment, is intervening in my life.

I, am made aware, the Lord God is always. Being who he says he is. And the Lord is always. Doing what he says he'll do. I am led by God, by the words of scripture. Often offering God's intervention to correct me.

I, am continually led to praise God, because I experience by correction his caring. Although the experience of being corrected. At the moment is not altogether joyful, I am thankful, the Lord is always faithful to fulfill his word.

Active And Alert:

The Lord God, has proven to me, that he as Lord of my life. Is an alert, and active participant. I feel loved, and blessed by the privilege of seeking, and knowing, the working of the Lord.

The Lord God has clearly shown me, He is able and faithful, to intervene. And the Lord faithfully redirects my thoughts, and my actions, by his word:

The Lord's Track Record:

Our Lord God, has a beautiful soul restoring tract record. God's word testifies by promises given, and kept. The Lord devotedly accomplishes his purpose.

The accomplishment of the Lord God's purpose. Has been confirmed in his word. The promises of the Lord is seen, in the lives of his trusting servants.

Nothing the Lord God, has encouraged for me to follow, has wasted my time. The way for my soul to know, and overcome sin. Is well established in Christ.

Well Done Before:

I, rejoice that before the world began. Salvation through the Lord Christ Jesus, was fully established for fulfillment.

In the spirit, I, see, and claim. I am being prepared for Christ's kingdom. By God's faithful living, and word, I emerge for righteousness sake.

By the sealing of God's Holy Spirit. I am declared by Christ to be his. It is by the Holy Spirit that I know I, am eternally sealed.

And I, know I, am set apart (sanctified). To live, and to minister. For the Lord God's, soul, blessing purpose.

I, understand by the word that I, am washed, sanctified, and justified in Christ. And by the Holy Spirit I am led to trust, teach, and exalt Christ Jesus.

In order to be blessed, I, know I, need to serve. And to rejoice in the work of God's salvation. I thrive in recalling the Lord God's track record, is that which has prepared me:

> "…ye are **washed**, but ye are **sanctified**, but ye are **justified in the name of the Lord Jesus**, and **by the Spirit of our God.** 1 Corinthians 6:11"

> "Unto the church of God…to them that are **sanctified in Christ Jesus, called to be saints**, with all that in every place **call upon the name of Jesus Christ** our Lord, both theirs and ours: **Grace be unto you, and peace, from God our Father, and from the Lord Jesus Christ**. I thank my

God always on your behalf, for **the grace of God which is given you by Jesus Christ**; That **in everything ye are enriched by him, in all utterance, and in all knowledge**;

Even as **the testimony of Christ was confirmed in you**: So that ye come behind in no gift; waiting for the coming of our Lord Jesus Christ: 1 Corinthians 1:2-7"

Revelations:

Based upon Christ manifesting his ability, to know and help me. I have learned with fulfilled assurance I, am complete in Christ. I, have revelations of assurance from the righteous, life of Christ Jesus.

I, have learned to pay attention to the Lord Christ's words. And I, have learned to pay special attention to Christ's life example.

I, understand by Christ's, life example I, am being led to know, and acknowledge God's love.

I, find the way I, am to love, and lead others to love, is fully identified in the life of Christ. Without a doubt I know the way to all blessings resides in Christ.

To have a clear and sure way to salvation, God gave his Son. The Lord Christ Jesus, is God's perfect manifestation of love.

Christ represents all that the Father has declared himself to be. And clarifies all that he planned for man to become. To have as promised life eternal by inheritance with Christ. Includes a blessed, and thriving life, in Christ here and now.

Planned Guidance:

Christ Jesus, I see is God's plan to guide all mankind. Following Christ, I, am led to desire, and to obtain God's holy, and perfect likeness.

Christ to me is the gracious expression of his Father's perfect love. Christ Jesus from the beginning was sent with the life-giving provisions.

Every step Christ made, was for guiding all of mankind into seeking his kingdom. And to desire his righteousness, above all desires.

By Christ's sacrificial, submissive, love. I was led to understand love, is doing the will of the Father. Because of the love of the Father, Christ was sent.

Christ was sent, to be the good shepherd of the soul. Christ's life as my good shepherd, and his words of truth, keep me on tract. Following Christ, I, am led to seek the will of the Father:

"I can of mine own self do nothing: as I hear, I judge: and my judgment is just; because **I seek not mine own will, but the will of the Father which hath sent me.** John 5:30"

Life Giving Light:

By the true light being displayed in Christ's life. I, am set free from the world's constant evolving, and established darkness. A most important direction Christ Jesus gave. Is for his followers, to love, and obey him, for his Father's glory.

I, see as Christ my Lord, was in heart, mind, and spirit, submitted to his Father. Is the way I, am led to submit in love, and obedience to Christ, for the Father's glory.

Just as Christ Jesus cherished, and lived by every word of God. I, know I am privileged. To cherish, and live by every word of God.

Christ Jesus leads me to know, and share the doctrine he shared. Same as he obeyed, and shared his Father's doctrine.

I, learned to cherish the opportunity, to share Christ. I, rejoice in the help given by God, for me to follow, and share Christ. I, strive to make known God's words of truth. Truth is verified in the deeds of Christ Jesus.

Through the Father's love, Christ Jesus, was sent for man to know. and live Christ's commands. The blessings attached to achieving Christ's kingdom.

I, see the ways to the kingdom of God. Is the love paved way demonstrated. By the Lord Christ's, willing submission. In the life example of Christ my Lord.

I, see the way to all goodness, righteousness, and truth. Is verified, and obtained by abiding in submission, same as Christ.

No-other:

Christ Jesus, as my Lord, fully leads the way, for me, to live. As I, am led by Christ Jesus. To know, and understand the way of truth, and righteousness.

I, find relief in knowing I am not, to commit my life to follow any carnal man. Following the Lord Christ Jesus. I am free from vain worship.

Worship to me is not true, that exalts any person or organization of man, with Christ. I, cling to Christ, as my kinsman, redeemer, and so much more.

Looking To Christ Avoids Uplifting Man:

I, look to Christ Jesus, as the only way to the Father. Following Christ, by studying God's purpose from his life. Keeps me looking to Christ for direction.

To go in the path the Lord Christ set before me. Is the way I, know shall give glory to the Father.

By the Lord God's grace, I am committed, to know, and follow Christ Jesus. It is by Christ's grace that I, do not ever need to commit myself to trust mankind:

> "But Jesus **did not commit himself unto them, because he knew all men**, And needed not that any should testify of man: for **he knew what was in man**. John 2:24-25"

> "Neither is there salvation in any other: for **there is none other name under heaven given** among men, whereby we must be saved. Acts 4:12"

> "For **other foundation can no man lay** than that is laid, which is Jesus Christ. 1 Corinthians 3:11"

Taught By His Spirit:

I, find Christ can, and does intervene, by his Holy Spirit. The Holy Spirit always teaches with the word. The fruit, gifts, and presence of the Holy Spirit. Keeps me maturing in my Christ.

Christ Jesus has manifested God the Father's love. I, know the constant soul reviving work of the Holy Spirit. Keeps me connected with Christ Jesus.

I, am led by the Holy Spirit. To remember the words, and deeds of Christ Jesus. And in this way, truth, is being built into my life.

> "But the Comforter, which is the Holy Ghost, whom the Father will send in my name, **he shall teach you all things, and bring all things to your remembrance, whatsoever I have said unto you.** John 14:26"

> "Even the **Spirit of truth**; whom the world cannot receive, because it seeth him not, neither knoweth him: but **I will not leave you comfortless**: I will come to you. John 14:17-18"

I, feel blessed to know I, am accompanied through life. By the Holy Spirit's teaching presence. The presence of the Holy Spirit, is always present. The integrity, wisdom, knowledge, and understanding of God accompanies the Holy Spirit.

I am so blessed, and comforted, as I, claim, and accept God's ever-present help. to live God's truth. I, feel the Spirit of truth, is there to give me guidance, and I, often rejoice.

I, know without a doubt that I, am indwelt by the comforter. By the Holy Spirit, I have a live-in teacher, and Christ, honoring encourager.

Led To Consider Others:

I find having firm trust in the Lord God's presence by the Holy Spirit. Is that which leads in considering other people.

It is by the Lord knowing I, would need help, for teaching, and guiding others. The Holy Spirit was planned to teach, and lead me in teaching, others.

It is also for the compassionate treatment of others, that I, am endowed by the Holy Spirit. I, know I, am sealed by God's Holy Spirit with purpose.

To know the love-based actions, I, am to have, towards all members of mankind. I, have guidance. By God's Holy Spirit, I, am taught, to know Christ. To Know Christ, is to know his love, and care for all mankind.

In my relationship towards mankind. I, know I live, to be spiritual salt, and light. And as a witness of Christ's merciful work. I, know Christ's love, is to be manifested through me.

Purpose Of My Life:

To testify to others of Christ being the light of life. Is the purpose the Lord has for my life. It is by the Holy Spirit that I, am able to focus on the life example of Christ, towards others,

Blessing friends, and foes is a priority. To direct my life, for seeing others by Christ's merciful eyes. Is my soul's priority. By committing myself as planned by the Father. To the Lord Christ Jesus. I am determined, to obediently, remain in the purposeful, study of God's word.

And by relying upon the Holy Spirit. I follow God the Father's plea, to hear his Son. And by obedience, I, am enabled by the Holy Spirit, to manifest the life of Christ, to others:

> "And there came a voice out of the cloud, saying, **This is my beloved Son: hear him.** Luke 9:35"

> "Hath in these last days **spoken unto us by his Son**, whom he hath appointed heir of all things, by whom also he made the worlds; Hebrews 1:2"

> "But **unto the Son he saith, Thy throne, O God, is for ever** and ever: a **sceptre of righteousness** is the sceptre of thy kingdom. **Thou hast loved righteousness,** and **hated iniquity**; therefore God, even thy **God, hath anointed thee** with the **oil of gladness** above thy fellows. Hebrews 1:8-9"

The Father Adds And Strengthens:

The Father is identified as the one who adds to the church. And promotes growth in Christ's, church. It is for the growth of Christ's church. That the Father takes continual actions. By his chastening, and comforting role:

> "I am the true vine, and **my Father** is the husbandman. Every **branch in me that beareth not fruit he taketh away:**

and every **branch that beareth fruit, he purgeth it**, that it may bring forth more fruit John 15:1-2."

Chapter 2

NOTED TROUBLE

I, was soon led, to have disappointment, from the SDA church, where we, currently had membership. After my zeal, and burning desire to be a faithful servant of Christ, by using God's word, for truth.

With desire to better exalt the truth of Christ. I, had increased my time and knowledge of God's word. I, focused on being able to identify, the truth of God's word, by what Christ lived, and taught.

Attitude Of Resistance:

I, was meet with passive resistance, by many accepted as dedicated, and knowledgeable, SDA church leaders. I, by observation, was led to realize. God's word was not honored.

I, did not see the word of God. Was honored with the authority given by God. I recognized observed a subtle resistance. To the full use of God's word.

The word not upheld by the leaders. Was a disappointment. The lack of enthusiasm for Christ. As leader of the church. I, identified was seriously missing.

Though leading members of the SDA church. Appeared to take pleasure in claiming the church had the truth. We saw there was an effort to promote, another gospel.

A different focus, was communicated during worship. A practice, of denomination exalting. And a person of the past. Caused Christ the true head of his church. Appearing as one, just along for the ride.

The removal of Christ. From his rightful leadership place. The place planned and given by his Father. Before the world began. Allowed the writings of mankind. To appear as authority.

With another name being spoken. And another word being exalted. Discrepancies were evident. There was the blatant God's word as the only. Written source of truth was watered down. With God's word down played. It was in essence replaced.

The word unchanging word of God. Emphasizing Christ's lead in all issues was missing. And it caused me to see. There was a presence of darkness. That was vainly making attempts. To block the true light.

Longing For Christ:

One of the things I, am blessed to identify. When I, connected with God's Holy Spirit. I, longed for seeing Christ. Exalted in his place in the church. As I, see him presented, in God's word.

A passion for seeing, and establishing. Christ above all, in every lesson. Was my purpose, and joy. To share how Christ was made known. By his Father, as the only blessed head. And leader of his church.

It was to me a blessed pleasure. Promised by the faithful Father. Taught, and commissioned by Christ. The longing for God's word, uplifting Christ. To have the preeminence in every presented subject. Was fully identified, and established in my ministry efforts.

Mighty In Truth:

The Lord God by the Holy Spirit teaching the word of God. Has established in me, zeal for the Lord. Increasing my desire in knowing Christ. Who by his life opened the door to truth.

In sharing God's word, in honor of Christ Jesus. It also increased my pleasure. In identifying Christ's pre-determined role. I, magnify, and seek to walk in, the Lord's revealed righteousness. For the exposure, and removal of sin. Christ needs to be recognized.

> "For he **put on righteousness as a breastplate**, and an **helmet of salvation** upon his head; and he put on the **garments of vengeance** for clothing, **and was clad with zeal as a cloke**. Isaiah 59:17"

> "John answered, saying unto them all, I indeed baptize you with water; but **one mightier than I cometh**, the latchet of whose shoes I am not worthy to unloose: **he shall baptize you with the Holy Ghost and with fire:** Luke 3:16"

"For **every one shall be salted with fire,** and every sacrifice shall be salted with salt. Mark 9:49"

Zeal Of Love:

There is in God's word, a promise of zeal. That would go along with, the sealing of the Holy Spirit. It blesses me, to consider how the life of zeal in Christ works.

Truth was lived unwaveringly, by Christ Jesus. Being sent to take on the flesh of man. Christ was prepared because of his Father's anointing, by the Spirit. And by the Father, who sent him, being with him.

The Father, Son, and Holy Spirit, being one together. Identifies God's will for us, to be one with them, in love. Christ's gospel is all based on love:

> "And **he that sent me is with me**: the Father hath not left me alone; for **I do always those things that please him.** John 8:29"

> "Now before the feast of the passover, when Jesus knew that his hour was come that he should depart out of this world unto the Father, **having loved his own which were in the world, he loved them unto the end.** John 13:1"

> "But that the world may know that I love the Father; and **as the Father gave me commandment, even so I do…** John 14:31"

"For even **hereunto were ye called**: because Christ also suffered for us, leaving us an example, **that ye should follow his steps: Who did no sin, neither was guile found in his mouth:** 1 Peter 2:21-22"

Word Of God Resisted:

I, sadly discovered, I, was not in agreement with many leaders, of the current SDA denomination. Though leaders, in the new church claimed they were believing, teaching, and following the truth.

The current SDA denomination according to Scriptures. I, could see was not giving truth. From the knowledge I, gained I, identified the truth of Christ's life.

Christ lived and promoted the doctrine as given from the beginning. What Christ lived, and taught, was, and is my determination:

I, am maturing to enjoy blessing the Lord God. I, sought, and found ways to make sure by Christ's leading. Christ's word, and his ways was made known.

Whatever I, shared when I, ministered, had to be in accord to what Christ Jesus lived, and taught. I, needed others to know my sharing is for Christ. And is in harmony with the life Christ lived.

To live by every word of God, as Christ taught, became my focus. The Lord God's word, was, and remains, my constant revelation for truth. The life lived, and the teaching by Christ. Is my focus above any denominational doctrine, and leading of man.

Upholding The Word:

Exalting God's word, I, was sorry to find, my effort was not appreciated. By illuminating the word, of God. I, did not please many claiming to be leaders of the true church.

Because I, saw Christ as my only true righteous leader. I, sought and still seek, to learn as scripture prophesied, from Christ's teaching life.

I, settled it in my heart, that my purpose. Must be directed by truth. Christ's leading became my focus. I, pursued following Christ, by seeking and highlighting. God's word, during all my ministering, and congregational worship.

God's word as it was presented. And illuminated by the life of Christ Jesus. Became first in my choices for ministry. My, passion remains to follow Christ Jesus' leading, as my Lord. As I, was led, and commanded, by Christ, in the word.

Using God's word, has increased my comfort. I, have continually received comfort. From the words and Life of Christ Jesus. I, have instructions that give me peace. Even in the face of opposition:

> **"Remember the word that I said unto you**, The servant is not greater than his lord. If they have persecuted me, they will also persecute you; **if they have kept my saying, they will keep yours also.** John 15:20"

> **"My sheep hear my voice**, and I know them, and **they follow me:** John 10:27"

> "**that the world may know that I love the Father;** and as the **Father gave me commandment, even so I do.** Arise, let us go hence. John 14:31"

Uplifting Christ Lacking:

I, learned by up close observation. That many people saying they are Christians. In many all denominations. Also walk in the same self-preaching. And denomination promoting manner.

Too often I, find many are devoted in, and outside of church. To preaching, and promoting themselves. Without dedication to following Christ, and making Christ known. The gospel of Christ, as commissioned, and lived by Christ, is this very day being neglected.

Scripture Sharing:

I, have shared scripture verses from the bible, with far too many claiming Christianity. Who were completely unaware of what Christ taught. There are many important subjects Christ Jesus lived, and taught. There are commands of Christ omitted by too many Christians, Who delight in following vain man.

Christ as head of the church, is often not stressed. Or encouraged by Christian leaders. And it is far too often that praise is given to a Pastor. Or other church leaders of man. Man is being exalted as being the one providing salvation.

Not having elementary knowledge of Christ. By those saying they are Christian. Is found to be common. Giving others encouragement, to hear, and share the Lord God's word. Was, and shall remain my, priority.

It is my priority in living my life. To live according to the way the Lord Christ directed his disciples to observe, and teach. Preaching, and exalting Christ. Is the utmost purpose of my worship, and ministry.

Encouraged By Rejection:

Rejection for my use of God's word. Became for me a spiritual gain. Disapproval for my use of God's word. Increased my word of God.

From desire and hunger, I, crave knowledge from God's word. More knowledge of the Lord God, and his ways is my passion because I, see the lack, and result of that, which is lacking.

Increasing my interest in God's word, also worked from observing stagnation. And my desire, is working to increase. Other's interest in God's word.

By going to the scriptures regarding current world events. Helped me to treasure the Lord God's counsels so much more.

Learning more of an event by subject. Helped me become more appreciative of the Lord Jesus.

Choosing to make God known more. I, realized resides in sharing Christ. Christ's leadership, needing restoration, increases my purpose for sharing God's word.

Joy Enhanced By Service:

Working in church ministry positions, which I had very joyfully accepted (Communication Sec, Sabbath School Sec. Ass, Deaf

Ministries). Blessed me with the opportunities to often, share God's word. I, still look forward to searching, and sharing God's word, every day.

By having the desire to serve the Lord God. I, increased my time with hearing the word of God by using the audio, KJV bible readings, by Alexander Scourby.

I daily, prayerfully search God's word to actively praise God, and to prepare to bless the lives of others, and myself.

I actively used God's word in the SDA denomination before leaving.

Because I, had accepted various ministry positions. In regular practice of using God's word. I, increasingly found pleasure in using God's word. To which I, am now dedicated.

God's word became, and remains my delight. In serving the Lord Christ Jesus. I, learned I, truly needed to look to the Lord, for his, guidance. I, also learned I, needed to depend upon Christ to guide me, in all my, leadership roles.

I soon realized by actively using God's word, I created a noted displeasure. My enthusiastic use of bible scripture, and Christ's example offended. Use of God's word did not, and does not please many church leaders.

As I, serve Christ, the word replaces. the false doctrine, that is taught by man. False doctrine, is used by many major church organizations.

Christ himself is rejected, by church leaders denying. And rejecting the commandments of Christ. That are clearly spoken by Christ, in the word of God. And commanded to be followed.

Discernment From Christ:

I, trusted in Christ Jesus for leading me. In relationship to the oppositions of others. When it, became noted, by me there was not the same passion for God's word, by SDA denomination leaders. It was easily identified that subtle resentment was present.

In the practice, of many of the church leaders. It became very evident there was a divide. My purpose of using the word of God to serve God, was not supported.

I, soon realized in the SDA denomination. God's word being used was in constant conflict. With the words of some SDA church leaders. There was the devoted quoting, and exalting another source, being upheld as truth.

It became evident to me that my, practice of magnifying Christ Jesus, and God's word, was resented. Not supporting the church leader's practice. Appeared to threaten the church leadership's firmly set agenda.

Effort To Walk As led By Christ:

Though we were members of the same. SDA Church denomination we had transferred from. The practice in worship, was not the same.

So different was the practice of the current church. It was not the same as the same SDA church denomination, my husband, and I, had transferred from.

It became an undeniable reality. The current church, had a much different ministry focus than the one, we had left in CA, when we moved away.

Demonstrated in subtle ways, and some right-out scripture denying ways. Was effort to put someone else in Christ's place, as head, and having all authority. There were efforts to over-ride the scripture magnifying Christ, as being the everlasting gospel. Was pointing out for worship,

Our efforts remain, to hold-up Christ as being head of all things. And Christ having the preeminence in all subjects to the church. To restrict, and limit the practice of our ministry efforts. There was noted interference.

We were led to recognize our efforts in serving Christ, were not welcome. It was soon recognized, by some noted interference, and some comments, such as, 'new people coming in, and trying to take over'.

We were not in harmony with the current SDA denomination leadership. By not having the same purpose as the church leaders. We had to face the reality of the situation.

Bob and I, were by wisdom prompted to depart from the denomination. When going to worship anywhere. We now are more attentive to a church's self-promoting practice.

Awareness of Purpose:

Observing carefully the practices of all churches we attend. Keeps us from becoming members of any church. Though, we, enjoy worshipping the Lord with congregational praise. We are aware we can avoid doctrinal issues by attending a church just to worship.

At any church we attend, we now give consideration to the part we have control over. To have proper worship, requires us to have an abiding relationship with our Lord.

Worshipping for us is to seek to maintain, and build an abiding relationship with Christ. Focusing on Christ's doctrine, and his pattern in worship, directs our worship focus.

Whenever we attend any church for worship, our focus is simply to worship the Lord. Our focus is on worshipping Christ, And glorifying God the Father.

To abide in Christ Jesus, and exalting, Christ's deserved leadership is our delight. Enjoyment at any church, for us. Is to attend with purposeful determination to bless the Lord.

To encourage others to grow. In blessing the Lord Jesus is a delight. The need to follow Christ Jesus example in worship. Increases the use of God's word in my daily life.

My maturity in ministry increased, as the importance of God's word increased. My efforts to use God's word continue to grow in bringing me comfort, and contentment.

From what the Lord had set before me. By my contact at, and away from the church. I remain in soul transformation growth. By attending upon God's word. I, find great satisfaction and blessings, in pursuing Christ.

To spread God's word publicly I, was at one time creating, and distributing. Laminated, Bookmarks, calendars, and other bible verse, sources. For some persons receiving the created items it became a special treasure.

And I, occasionally have contact with individuals who share. They still have a bookmark that was, and is a special blessing to their life.

> "The Lord **hath done great things for us**; whereof we are glad. Psalms 126:3"

> "**My praise shall be of thee** in the great congregation: I will pay my vows before them that fear him. Psalm 22:25"

> "**I will give thee thanks in the great congregation: I will praise thee among much people.** Psalm 35:18"

> "**I have preached righteousness** in the great congregation: lo, I have not refrained my lips, O Lord, thou knowest. Psalm 40:9"

CHAPTER 3

APPRECIATING GOD

Special God Intervening Moments: It was early in the morning of February 29th, 2000, when I was preparing a news-letter. I had as Communication Sec created the news-letter, "Visions & Voices", for enhancing worship efforts at the church,

Suddenly on that special day, there was a sudden interruption. A quiet, and silent voice, was heard in my spirit saying, "Marciel". I remembered the name, Marciel, was of a young expectant mother, who should soon be delivered of her baby.

Because of the prompting I had received in my spirit. I, immediately called Pastor Dixon's home. I, immediately had contact with Pastor Dixon.

Pastor Dixon sounding very exhausted. Informed me of the delivery difficulty of Marciel. Pastor Dixon also shared how prayer had been going on all night, for Marciel.

It was shared that there had been long tiring hours of prayer. There had been prayers initiated by the church, with no progress. I, was informed that Marciel, was presently at the hospital, and they were planning a cesarian.

With tiredness in his voice, Pastor Dixon shared how Marciel's difficulty had only advanced. Pastor Dixon shared, how the doctors were planning at that moment, to use surgery, to remove Marciel's baby.

Seeking The Lord To Turn Things Around:

Pastor Dixon gave me a hospital number. Where, I was able to make immediate contact with the husband. As I, was led to take on the burden of Marciel, and her unborn, I, first called Rita Price, at Family Life Radio.

To allow dedicated prayer warriors, to hear the broadcast, and be in agreement for Marciel, and her unborn. I, initiated spiritual contact for Marciel's situation.

I felt confident the decision to have Marciel's situation announced to prayer warriors around the country, was the Lord God's desire:

> "Bear ye one another's burdens, and so fulfil the law of Christ. Galatians 6:2"

One the fascinating things concerning my contact with Rita Price. The announcer Carl Jackson, who was the one who broadcasted, and presented prayers for prayer warriors. And Carl who prayed himself for specific needs, had already gone into the broadcast studio (red-light on).

And the studio door was closed (Rita regrettably communicated) that the message could not be given to Carl. While Rita was stating prayer would still be offered for Marciel, and her unborn infant. There suddenly there was a change,

Rita Price, with a very excited and gleeful voice, said, 'wait Carl has come out of the studio' (something which normally never happened). Carl Jackson receiving the request for Marciel, resulted in allowing Carl Jackson, along with a visiting Pastor, to pray on radio, which allowed the involvement of prayer warriors.

I, later learned many prayer warriors from hearing the prayer, with the appeal, supported the effort. There was also gleeful thanksgiving expressed at the radio station. It was identified, the Lord, had his part in the overall broadcast, and prayers for Marciel, and her baby.

Seeing God Blessing:

I, made contact by phone with Marciel's husband Terrel Williams, who was waiting at the hospital. I let Terrel know prayer warriors would be joining in prayer with Carl Jackson.

The father was in the spirit of trusting the Lord, on behalf of his wife, Marciel, and their unborn baby. There was no AM radio available, for use at the hospital (that would allow Terrel to hear the praying of Carl Jackson, and a visiting Pastor).

Terrel, at the hospital, and I at home, prayed together. I, remember the prayers that we were inspired to pray, included the offering of thanksgiving for God's mercy, and constant care:

> "**O give thanks unto the Lord**; for he is good; for **his mercy endureth for ever**. 1 Chronicles 16:34"

Our God Is Awesome:

The father of a baby girl, 'Aaliyah', a leap year baby, rejoiced as he later shared with me. In essence, how the doctors, and nurses all prepared to perform surgery were dismayed.

Natural birth occurred right before their eyes. It was, and is a joy felt even now. To remember hearing from the father how the medical team, were in awe, from the Lord God's merciful working.

The medical team witnessed Marciel, deliver her baby daughter, 'Aaliyah' normally. It could not be denied, the normal delivery, of 'Aaliyah' (as God willed) happened, immediately after prayer.

Unforgettable Lesson Of Mercy:

As I considered the lessons the Lord God, includes in all his working. I ask myself, what did you learn? I, am filled with awe, as I recognize the Lord God, truly does love. And how the Lord is compassionately involved with 'the least of these'.

From that special attention the Lord afforded an unborn baby girl, I wonder today, 'what shall Aaliyah inspire to be?' There were praises at 0Family Life Radio that day, and days following. As the Lord's merciful kindness was shared.

I, am awed over the Lord's constant show of mercy. and the Lord God being forever recognized with many praises, for who he is, and what he does as the great 'I AM'.

Joy Sharing Of God's Work:

The following is what I wrote in 'Vision & Voices' the churches news-letter, regarding the Williams family's experience. (included was a picture of a teddy bear)

PARENTING

On 2/29/00, Terrel and Sis Marciel Williams, became parents. There was more than the usual concern by Bro Williams for his baby daughter who was not yet born, and a demonstration of tender expression for the mother.

His wife Marciel was having difficulty in labor, to the point of having doctors make a decision to take drastic measures.

Bro Williams knelt in prayer for the Lord's intervention. The Lord heard his prayer and soon others were joining in from all over the nation. God gave relief, and soon Aaliyah Williams was born:

My Special Prayer For Aaliyah:

> "By thee have I been **holden up from the womb**: thou art he that took me out of my mother's bowels: **my praise shall be continually of thee**. I am as **a wonder unto many;** but **thou art my strong refuge**. Let my mouth be filled with **thy praise and with thy honour all the day**. Psalms 71:6-8" Amen!

The Lord's Intervenes:

I had the experience of being prompted in my spirit on a 5th day of the week. To go to the bible book store, and purchase a song.

I, purchased a song that had accompanying music for performance included. "That's How Much I Love You", by Kathy Troccoli, was the song I selected. Even though I, at the time for some reason, was not particularly fond of the song.

I, felt it was an okay, song. and it was purchased. I, started learning the song, and heard the song differently. As I, practiced the song, it was for me a real blessing. The song agreed with, and magnified God, and God's word.

Spirit Led Preparation:

I was in the shower early on the following, (Sabbath) 7th day morning, in preparation for attending church. In the midst of my shower I, heard in my spirit a prompting, to take the song I had recently purchased, to church with me.

I, can never forget my husband Bob's, astonished look, and response when, I, told him I, was to take the song, because there was not planned to be any music.

My husband said, "what!? there always is music". Bob, also looked a bit puzzled over my discloser, of 'being told'. I, responded to the message I, received in my spirit. I, took the song, 'That's How Much I Love You,' with me.

At the time music was to occur in the service before the sermon, it was noted the music presenter was not there. The head elder, Charles Loadholt, after there was an unusual silence, rose from his seat and stood near the altar.

Charles Loadholt with a puzzled, and with a questioning expression on his face, asked the question, "does anyone have any music!?"

My husband Bob was acting as deacon that day, was seated with other deacons on the front pew. While, I sat on the first seat in a middle row.

I, hesitated with my response, and Bob told me later, he was thinking, 'Oh no'. Bob, felt anxious, because, Bob never had a spiritual experience, such as what was occurring at that moment.

Bob was a bit overwhelmed by what he was experiencing. To Bob it was seeing, prophesy happen at that very moment. "I have a song" was my response, to Elder Charles Loadholt.

I immediately took the performance tape, to the one on hand for playing the accompanying tape. It took no time to locate the appropriate spot on the tape, and I returned to the sanctuary.

I approached the usual place for a solo singer to stand, by the altar. And suddenly the song I had not at the first been fond of, I specially loved.

As, I sang the song, 'That's How Much I Love You,'. In my heart, and spirit, I, felt blessed, as I, recognized Christ, and his work was communicated, in every part of the following song:

That's How Much I Love You, By Kathy Troccoli:

"I died for you I'd do it all again if I had to. To show you what you really mean to me. I cried for you I hung on the cross so you wouldn't have to I made a way to set your spirit free.

That's how much I love you. That's how much I want you to see

You are My child and you mean so much to me. I gave you the stars, the sun, the moon, yes, I went that far So no matter where you would go, you think of me.

The mountain's fair, the beautiful oceans are there to remind you. That I can satisfy your every need. That's how much I love you That's how much I want you to see. That you are My child and you mean so much to me. You are My child and you mean so much to me."

The added blessing of the song," That's How Much I Love You." was that it was a perfect fit for the message that was given. And another blessing, regarding music, for that Sabbath day.

After my singing, a man walked, into the sanctuary, no one knew, and the unknown man had a song to share. The Lord God had provided a perfect intervention.

The Lord had provided the music, which would not have happened that day. There always had been two special, musical presentations. One presentation as usual was expected, before the sermon that was presented by me.

And, an unknown man making a request to sing, provided the song following the sermon. The remarkable thing about the songs chosen unaware. The songs both were in harmony with the sermon.

Makes His Works Known:

I, find there is a building up, of trust in my spirit, from having part in God's the work of God. The treasure of the Lord God's, great and marvelous working, awes me.

I, find the Lord God works according to all his promises. All the Lord God's promises, and my experience with him. I know all promises are fulfilled as proclaimed in the word of God. All promises have reliance due to the awesome truth of Christ Jesus:

> "**Great and marvellous are thy works,** Lord God Almighty; **just and true are thy ways,** thou King of saints…Who shall not fear thee, O Lord, and glorify thy name? for thou only art holy: for **all nations shall come and worship before thee; for thy judgments are made manifest**. Revelation 15:3-4"

> "**The eternal God is thy refuge,** and **underneath are the everlasting arms**… Deuteronomy 33:27"

Visions And Voices:

The first monthly newsletter was issued at the church on the 30th of March of 1996, and mailings also went to those home-bound, and prison bound. I can testify the newsletter, Visions and Voices, was used powerfully by the Lord.

Not only did the newsletter, I, was inspired to create inspire me, 'Vision And Voices', inspired others also. I received reports of how articles, and even the children activities (adults also looked forward to), did give comfort, strength, and encouragement.

I could see how, the Lord was using the monthly newsletter, 'Vision And Voices' to foster positive God honoring life choices. From some receiving, 'Visions and Voices' at home, there was an immediate positive response. That took many by surprise.

There was with the receiving of the 'Vision, And Voices', immediate positive response, where there had been no contact. With many of the shut-in members paying, tithes, and giving offerings, by mail happened, without expectation.

'Visions and Voices', basically became a way to say to those not attending church that they were thought of, and loved. We, know it was by the Lord caring for the ones we were serving. To know that even in their absence, God loved them.

Ministering to missing members by, new-letters became a treasure to them. Being cherished, and cared for by the Lord, became more easily communicated. By the contact being made by news-letters.

The variety of sections of, 'Visions And Voices', said to us, who were led to create the sections of the newsletter. The Lord loves, and cares about our growth.

By scripture, I, see the Lord, is to be followed. And exalted, in all areas of our soul (body, heart/mind, and spirit). And in every area, due to sin. There needs to be a strengthening. To allow growth, in serving the Lord.

The newsletter said to those unable to attend church regularly. Even though they did not have a regular presence at church they mattered. And that they were always present to the Lord.

Many persons, who were not church members also had access to the, 'Vision And Voices', newsletter. The sections, that the Lord led me to create, were Christ centered. And covered subjects that are present in all life events.

Sharing messages in the newsletter, 'Vision And Voices' became a very important way of ministering, to myself as I, ministered to others. I, focused on serving the Lord, first above all church agendas.

Through the use of the newsletter. I, was enabled to minister to present, church members. Along with considering those members, that were home, and prison, bound.

Family and friends were also included in the mail list of 'Vision And Voices' for distribution. Along with some casual Radio contact acquaintances:

The following is a writing I posted at the 2nd year anniversary of, 'Vision And Voices':

'Happy Anniversary (2yrs) Visions And Voices goal is to focus, and highlight events in a way that agrees with. "If there be any praise." For his honor and glory.'

The 'Vision And Voices' ended in 2001, when my husband and I left the Sharon SDA church. But I, still have all the issues that were distributed.

Titles Of Vision And Voices Sections:

Sections of 'Vision And Voices' were: 'God's Store House', 'Program Highlights', 'Food for Meditation', and 'Health Nugget'. Other subjects included: 'Strengthen your Brother', 'Marriage for Better and Best', 'Signs of the Times'.

Other Sections: 'All age Kids Page'. 'Parenting', 'Personal Ministry', and 'Singles' I, also provided a place, that honored birthdays, and special life events.

The Lord Who Exalts Himself:

I, realize the most important reason for serving the Lord God, is him. In any way I, choose with any opportunity that is offered. I, know my efforts are all about the Lord. And must of all. I, know what I, choose to do, shall always be about the Lord.

> "The **Lord gave the word**: great was the company of those that published it. Psalms 68:11"

> "In God will I praise his word: **in the Lord will I praise his word**. Psalms 56:10"

> "As ye know how **we exhorted and comforted and charged every one of you**, as a father doth his children, **That ye would walk worthy of God**, who hath called you unto his kingdom and glory.

> For this cause also thank we God without ceasing, because, when ye received the word of God which ye heard of us, ye received it **not as the word of men, but as it is in truth, the word of**

God, which effectually worketh also in you that believe. 1 Thessalonians 2:11-13"

"By him therefore **let us offer the sacrifice of praise to God continually,** that is, the fruit of our lips giving thanks to his name. Hebrews 13:15"

CHAPTER 4

KEEPING THE LORD BEFORE US

Over a period of time, we have been approached. To support a church by membership. But we learned all churches, expect members. To reverently join, and follow their doctrine.

Not being allowed by Christ's doctrine, to accept any other doctrine, we avoid membership. Staying with Christ's doctrine, has kept me, and my husband, Bob, from having membership in any church.

Though willing to accept participation in a church service. Not accepting a church's doctrine is a hindrance. We, cannot be willing to accept any teaching.

All portions of a doctrine of any church. Must for God's sake, lift-up Christ. According to bible scripture. It is by scripture that we are taught, how to sturdy scripture. And the one we trust. To teach us scripture:

> "Whom shall he teach knowledge? and whom shall he make to understand doctrine?... For precept must be upon

precept, precept upon precept; line upon line, line upon line; here a little, and there a little: Isaiah 28:9-10"

"Turn you at my reproof: behold, I will pour out my spirit unto you, I will make known my words unto you. Proverbs 1:23"

Christ's life practice, and his commands. Taught, and for us, to follow lived. The life lived by Christ. Must be our priority, for acceptance.

Christ is not the author of confusion. All subjects taught by man. Requires harmony with Christ. Christ, never changes. Any word that he, taught:

"**Search the scriptures**; for in them ye think ye have eternal life: and they are **they which testify of me**. John 5:39"

"Jesus **Christ the same** yesterday, and to day, and for ever. Hebrews 13:8"

All doctrine for us must be in harmony with Christ. Doctrines, not showing harmony with Christ. Leads us to, say, 'no' to church membership. Not having church membership. Enhanced our purpose to see Christ. In his rightful place. To be worshipped, and adored for his Father's cause:

"For God so loved the world, that **he gave his only begotten Son**, that whosoever believeth in him should not perish, but have everlasting life. John 3:16"

> "Beloved, if **God so loved us,** we ought also to love one another. 1 John 4:11"

> "He that committeth sin is of the devil; for the devil sinneth from the beginning. For this purpose **the Son of God was manifested, that he might destroy the works of the devil**. 1 John 3:8"

Searching all doctrine, in seeking for Christ. Worked in me, to promote more spiritual growth. In seeking, to know and share the Lord. By staying in tune, with Christ's example. And promoting God's word. I, am able to say I, have been. And I, am being blessed:

> "Thy words were found, and I did eat them; and **thy word was unto me the joy and rejoicing of mine heart:** for I am called by thy name, O Lord God of hosts. Jeremiah 15:16"

By-passing Joining Churches:

Seeing Christ as our main leader, and the word of God being taught, as Christ commanded. Has provided a steady spirt of growth. By staying committed to God. I, have emerged into prioritizing Christ.

By the word according to Christ, we are to live. It is my determination. That, by Christ's life, and the word of God. Is the way we are enabled to influence others. To worship, and direct their lives, always towards Christ:

> "To the law and to the testimony: if they speak not according to this word, it is because there is no light in them. Isaiah 8:20"

> "For **he whom God hath sent speaketh the words of God**: for God giveth not the Spirit by measure unto him. John 3:34"

Having Christ, as the head, and living word. I, am determined, to see Christ exalted, in all subjects. Passing over membership in churches. I, see Christ, as the Father's elect with grace.

It is only by the commands, and life of Christ. That we have, the clear way. God's way to salvation, was established in Christ. Before, any of man's organizations, were established. Christ, is forever the abiding way of truth, for salvation:

> "Behold my servant, whom I uphold; **mine elect, in whom my soul delighteth**; I have put my spirit upon him: he shall bring forth judgment to the Gentiles. Isaiah 42:1"

Christ provides us with opportunities. To influence others to consider their choices. Anyone with a leadership position, in a church. They are only by Christ, equipped to serve Christ:

> "**Shew me thy ways**, O Lord; **teach me thy paths. Lead me in thy truth, and teach me**: for thou art the God of my salvation; on thee do I wait all the day. Psalm 25:4-5"

Escape From Mankind's Doctrine:

There is always a problem in a church. When there is a conflict between what the leaders are preaching. And what God's word has to say, on same subject:

> "Thus shall ye say every one to his neighbour, and every one to his brother, **What hath the Lord answered?** and, **What hath the Lord spoken?** Jeremiah 23:35"

> "Thus shalt thou say to the prophet, **What hath the Lord answered thee?** and, **What hath the Lord spoken?** Jeremiah 23:37"

The Lord, gave me a bible verse, which gave me comfort since, my purpose is to serve him. In hearing something out of tune with God's word. I, put my trust in the Lord God's teaching. I, rejoice to find, in any situation, the Lord God has provided the truth:

> "Who is among you that feareth the Lord, that obeyeth the voice of his servant, that walketh in darkness, and hath no light? let him **trust in the name of the Lord, and stay upon his God.** Isaiah 50:10"

> "Concerning the works of men, **by the word of thy lips** I have **kept me** from the paths of the destroyer. Psalms 17:4"

Identifying Christ's Church body:

The Lord gave me great comfort. In leading me to the scripture verses. Which told me about the seal of God. Which is the Holy Spirit. Planned by the Father to add me to Christ's body.

> "He saith unto them, But whom say ye that I am? And Simon Peter answered and said, **Thou art the Christ, the Son of the living God.** And Jesus answered and said unto him, Blessed art thou, Simon Barjona: for **flesh and blood hath not revealed it unto thee, but my Father which is in**

heaven. And I say also unto thee, That thou art Peter, and upon this rock I will build my church; and the gates of hell shall not prevail against it. Matthew 16:15-18"

"The **Lord is my rock**, and **my fortress**, and **my deliverer;** my God, **my strength**, in whom I will trust; **my buckler**, and the horn of **my salvation**, and **my high tower**. Psalm 18:2"

"And they, **continuing daily with one accord in the temple,** and breaking bread from house to house, did eat their meat with gladness and singleness of heart, Praising God, and having favour with all the people. And **the Lord added to the church daily** such as should be saved. Acts 2:46-47"

"So then neither is he that planteth any thing, neither he that watereth; but **God that giveth the increase.** 1 Corinthians 3:7"

What Is Practiced In Churches:

My growing use of God's word as I, minister is to completely reconcile myself, and to God those I, with joy serve. I, recognize to follow Christ Jesus in congregation worship. Christ and the doctrine he taught must be Upheld regardless of the challenge.

I, have learned there is a heavier burden on man, by the word of man. Relief is given by God's word. That works on man. For man's complete soul. Using the word of God is something I, know is too often. In conflict with man created organizations.

There are organization leaders. That do not want any doctrinal change. That corrects, what they have without question, accepted. I, believe due to the religious practice, of mankind's organizations. Is the way mankind is caught up, in undesirable situations:

> "That this is a rebellious people, lying children, children that **will not hear the law of the Lord**: Which say to the seers, See not; and to the prophets, Prophesy not unto us right things, **speak unto us smooth things, prophesy deceits**: Get you out of the way, turn aside out of the path, **cause the Holy One of Israel to cease from before us.** Isaiah 30:9-11"

Pride Of Life Pit:

Having peer approval, and the determination. That your worship, is that specially chosen by God. Above all others is soul capturing.

It is only natural, to promote, and live. By what the chosen group has established. Is the truth for worship practice. Being spoken well of because the group is pleased. Is compromising, and soul defeating:

> "**Woe** unto you, **when all men shall speak well of you!** for so did their fathers to the false prophets. Luke 6:26"

At the first there are subtle, 'we' statements geared to control, a person's actions, to be in line with, their subtle influence. 'We, don't listen to others, because, we don't want to be confused', is one of the main 'we', statement, I, recall:

> "For **we dare not** make ourselves of the number, or **compare ourselves with some that commend themselves**: but **they measuring themselves** by themselves, and **comparing themselves** among themselves, **are not wise**. 2 Corinthians 10:12"

To make a man's words more important. Or equal with Christ's word's is an unprofitable vanity. Replacing Christ with man, is soul defeating. The devil's goal is to eliminate Christ.

All of the devil's lie infested, tricks. Are geared to remove Christ. Daily effort is employed, to remove God's word. Removal of God's word is an intentional effort of Satan.

To take the word of God away. Is purposed by the father of lies. Ignoring God's written word is suicide. Having Christ as, 'that prophet' it is the Father's continued will. That we hear Christ. Not hearing Christ's word. Leads to destruction:

> "For Moses truly said unto the fathers, **A prophet shall the Lord your God raise up** unto you **of your brethren**, like unto me; **him shall ye hear in all things** whatsoever he shall say unto you. And it shall come to pass, that **every soul, which will not hear that prophet, shall be destroyed** from among the people. Acts 3:22-23"

Correct information from God's word. Is the way we, correct our, ways. We live according to the information we accept. Denial is one of the subtle ways to keep people. From wanting to know Christ. Or from fully abiding in obedience to Christ.

I remind am reminded of the time of Christ, when religious leaders. With subtilty were discouraging people. From believing in the words of Christ. Or from spending any time listening to Christ:

> "Then came the officers to the chief priests and Pharisees; and they said unto them, **Why have ye not brought him?** The officers answered, Never man spake like this man. Then answered them the Pharisees, Are ye also deceived? **Have any of the rulers or of the Pharisees believed on him?** John 7:45-48"

Handling Finances For God:

Because of the consideration of God, being the one we serve. For Bob, in the role of treasurer. Dissatisfaction from Bob's judgement in denying funds requests occurred.

Bob, in his role as treasurer. Also received in essence, some boos, and humbugs. Bob, as treasurer considered his position, was serving God.

And same as all ministry positions. Required accountability to God. Bob, with reason, denied requests for funds. That were made by some ministry leaders.

Bob, determined, the use of the church funds. Had to be seen as serving a ministry need. To Bob, his role as treasurer, was to purposely fulfill, a ministry, need.

Treasurer, was a much needed, and sacred role. That demanded for Bob, to be faithful, and accountable. Bob, responded with denial. To requests he saw as red-flags.

Bob, identified some leaders in ministry positions. Felt no accountability was needed from them. Some leaders making requests for funds. Felt because they had put into the offering. They should be allowed, to receive the same amount, they had given.

Some felt free to get credit for giving. And then allowed freedom, to removal the funds. But Bob, said no, 'not on God's watch'.

Because accountability, had not been required before. Some leaders, demonstrated resentment. When they were asked to give account. 'Just coming in and trying to take over'. Was one noted expression of resentment. Bob remained accountable.

Purpose The Lord Gave Offends:

Many did, and do not take fondness. To how, I, was, and am led to fully thrust. My physical, mental, and spiritual energy. Into offering true worship, to the Lord God. I, understand, by God's provisions, I, am being led to exalt Christ Jesus, and his commands.

I gain comfort in feeling safe. In the way God gave for me to serve, him, in proclaiming Christ. My main purpose, is to clarify, that Christ is the one provided by the Father, to be heard, and followed. Christ the Lord, being seen as the living word. I, am content to be led by his word, and his, teaching Holy Spirit.

What the heavenly Father, Christ Jesus, and also his selected, mother, Mary. Had to say concerning the words of Christ Jesus, matters.

One of the things I, learned to appreciate concerning Christ. It cannot be denied. That by Christ using God's word, many are offended. And for that reason, the Father, made it known. Christ is to be heard:

> "…and behold a voice out of the cloud, which said, **This is my beloved Son**, in whom I am well pleased; **hear ye him**. Matthew 17:5"

> "His mother saith unto the servants, **Whatsoever he saith unto you, do it**. John 2:5"

> "And why call ye me, Lord, Lord, and do not the things which I say? **Whosoever cometh to me, and heareth my sayings, and doeth them**, I will shew you to whom he is like:

> **He is like a man which built an house, and digged deep, and laid the foundation on a rock**: and when the flood arose, the stream beat vehemently upon that house, and could not shake it: for it was founded upon a rock.

> But he that **heareth, and doeth not, is like a man that without a foundation built an house** upon the earth; against which the stream did beat vehemently, **and immediately it fell; and the ruin of that house was great.** Luke 6:46-49"

What Jesus Spoke Offends Sin:

As our light for directing our lives. The Lord Christ Jesus, spoke and lived truth. The Lord Christ Jesus is the promised way, the promised truth, and the promised light of life. Christ is to be heard, and followed.

And the Lord, has commanded his hearers, to live by every word of God. In using the word of God, Christ Jesus offended. And our Lord has called upon us to offend:

> "Sanctify the Lord of hosts himself; **and let him be your fear, and let him be your dread.** And he shall be for a sanctuary; but for a stone of stumbling and **for a rock of offence** to both the houses of Israel, for a gin and for a snare to the inhabitants of Jerusalem. Isaiah 8:13-1"

> "Therefore thus saith the Lord God, Behold, I lay in Zion **for a foundation** a stone, a **tried stone**, a **precious** corner stone, **a sure foundation**: he that believeth shall not make haste. Isaiah 28:16"

> "As it is written, Behold, I lay in Sion **a stumblingstone and rock of offence**: and whosoever **believeth on him shall not be ashamed.** Romans 9:33"

Authority To God's Word:

It is so important to me. That Christ Jesus commanded his hearers, To live by every word of God. I, have found God's word reveals God's grace, mercy, and the truth. In the word of Christ Jesus, is light, and it is his word.

It is by focusing on the identity of the Lord Christ. From the beginning, of scripture. That has given me clarity. It is by knowing the prophesies, and the life lived by Christ. That makes God's, word, the work of love. To restore the soul of mankind. Christ says the reason for error, is based upon not knowing God's word. God's word is to be known:

"And Jesus answering said unto them, Do ye not therefore err, **because ye know not the scriptures**, neither the power of God? Mark 12:24"

"And Jesus answered and said, while he taught in the temple, **How say the scribes** that Christ is the Son of David? **For David himself said by the Holy Ghost,** The Lord said to my Lord, Sit thou on my right hand, till I make thine enemies thy footstool. David therefore himself calleth him Lord; and whence is he then his son? **And the common people heard him gladly.** Mark 12:35-37"

"And because I tell you the truth, ye believe me not. Which of you convinceth me of sin? **And if I say the truth, why do ye not believe me?** John 8:45-46"

Lack Of Knowledge Leads To Hatred:

By not knowing God's love. And the Lord's disclosed purpose of love. And not seeing how. God treasures the soul of mankind. Hatred was stirred towards Christ Jesus.

Rather than going by the word of God. Leaders in Christ Jesus day. Leaned towards their own opinion. Or same as today, leaders accepted more readily. The opinion of other members of mankind. Which generally leads to hatred being practiced:

"Therefore the Jews sought the more to kill him, because he not only had broken the sabbath, but said also that God was his Father, making himself equal with God. John 5:18"

> "The Jews then murmured at him, because he said, I am the bread which came down from heaven. John 6:41"

We are kept in the state of disagreement over spiritual matters. Because the flesh lusts against the spirit. And mankind has by his sinful nature. A desire to receive approval from mankind. And for reason of desiring honor from man. Man tends to follow hard after mankind.

Seeking the leadership of mankind rather than acknowledging God, as leader. Is sorrowfully a soul stealing obstacle. Going by what man in a leadership position says. In place of knowing, and supporting the words of Christ. Naturally invokes, a life struggle.

Accepting God's word over mankind's. Calls for recognizing the difference. When led by God's word, which is also spirit. It is always going to be light against darkness.

It is noted that Christ confronted the religious leaders. That taught in his day. With the error of their doctrine. The doctrine differing from the word of God. Gives the devil an advantage.

Because the religious leaders were serving their own desires. They failed to see God's love in Christ:

> "Therefore said some of the Pharisees, This man is not of God, because he keepeth not the sabbath day. Others said, How can a man that is a sinner do such miracles? **And there was a division among them. John 9:16**"

Conflict In Doctrine:

There shall always remain, a conflict between God's word. Being held up, over the teaching of mankind. The main reason there is conflict is due to the devil. Who has an ongoing influence in the church. And in the preached doctrine, of mankind.

The world's church proclaims man's doctrine to be truth. Doctrines in error taught by man. Are designated as truth and ones giving the false doctrines are respected as the church's leaders.

With mankind believing it is the word of man. That the Lord God, desires to have mankind follow. Leaves doctrinal confusion, and false prophets in the churches:

> "**Let both grow together** until the harvest: and in the time of harvest I will say to the reapers, **Gather ye together first the tares, and bind them in bundles to burn them**: but gather the wheat into my barn. Matthew 13:30"

From The Beginning:

Listening to the Lord Christ Jesus. Is the Father's way from before the foundation of the world. The Son being appointed for mankind, from the beginning. Is the only way to truth, Because the Son same as the Father is the truth.

The Lord God has by prophesy prepared, a good, and perfect way. For mankind to know him by knowing his Son. It is by the word of God that we see Christ Jesus. Who reveals the working of the Father:

"God, who at sundry times and in divers manners spake in time past unto the fathers by the prophets, **Hath in these last days spoken unto us by his Son**, whom he hath appointed heir of all things, by whom also he made the worlds; Hebrews 1:1-2"

"**I will raise them up a Prophet from among their brethren**, like unto thee, and will put my words in his mouth; **and he shall speak unto them all that I shall command him.** Deuteronomy 18:18"

"Then those men, when they had seen the miracle that Jesus did, said, **This is of a truth that prophet that should come into the world.** John 6:14"

It is proven, following the words of Christ, will cause retaliation. Most of worship retaliation shall be prompted by leaders of mankind. Retaliation against truth is a sure and undeniable reality.

Prepared For What We Face:

In this world as the Lord proclaimed. Mankind is of few days filled with troubles. It is the Lord God, who prepares us. The Lord prepares to face. That, which we are moving towards. And needing for spiritual maturity to face.

If it is our purpose to honor the word of God. Christ teaches we are sent to live, and proclaim his word. I know I, shall continue to face some opposition, for Christ's sake.

Honoring the word of God, over the doctrine, and works of mankind. Opposition is actually what is to be experienced. When Christ, and the way of truth is chosen.

Nothing Other Than:

I, see according to God's word, there is no person, organization, or doctrine. Approved to stand in place of Christ Jesus. Being true followers, of the Lord Christ Jesus. We learn Christ, and God's word is truth.

By being fully devoted to proclaiming Christ Jesus, persecution follows. Persecution, and falsehood comes from man honoring, And man established institutions:

> "Blessed are they which are **persecuted for righteousness' sake:** for theirs is the kingdom of heaven. Blessed are ye, when men **shall revile you, and persecute you, and shall say all manner of evil against you falsely, for my sake.** Rejoice, and be exceeding glad: for great is your reward in heaven: for **so persecuted they the prophets which were before you.** Matthew 5:10-12"

> "Yea, and **all that will live godly in Christ** Jesus shall suffer persecution. 2 Timothy 3:12"

Contentment From Truth:

I, am content in recognizing, the Lord Christ Jesus. Is the only way, the only truth, and the only life to follow. Due to finding the Lord's faithfulness in keeping his promises. That is the reason why I, proclaim him:

> "**Blessed are they which are persecuted for righteousness' sake:** for theirs is the kingdom of heaven. Blessed are ye, when men shall revile you, and persecute you, and shall say all manner of evil against you falsely, for my sake. **Rejoice, and be exceeding glad: for great is your reward** in heaven: for so persecuted they the prophets which were before you. Matthew 5:10-12"

Even before the time of entering the heavenly kingdom, which shall be on the earth made new. I, look forward to the promises of the Lord. And I, experience promises are fulfilled. For those seeking Christ's kingdom, and looking. To claim the Lord's promised righteousness:

> "But **seek ye first** the **kingdom of God,** and **his righteousness**; and all these things shall be added unto you. Matthew 6:33"

> "Know ye not that **the unrighteous shall not inherit the kingdom of God?** Be not deceived: neither fornicators, nor idolaters, nor adulterers, nor effeminate, nor abusers of themselves with mankind, Nor thieves, nor covetous, nor drunkards, nor revilers, nor extortioners, shall inherit the kingdom of God. 1 Corinthians 6:9-10"

I, also consider the promises to those rejecting God's way. And I, want nothing to do with any way God rejects. The world's soul defeating darkness is exposed, because God is love.

Darkness Promotes Pride:

There is with darkness, the prideful need to resist humility. Since humility is needed to confess one's own sinful condition.

Anyone not accepting the gospel, by Christ. Are sorrowfully rejecting God.

Due to defying the truth the lack of humility is evident. By pride man is led. To be ashamed of the gospel. To be ashamed of the gospel of Christ, always promotes pride:

> "For **whosoever shall be ashamed of me and of my words, of him shall the Son of man be ashamed**, when he shall come in his own glory, and in his Father's, and of the holy angels. Luke 9:26"

> "For all that is in the world, the lust of the flesh, and the lust of the eyes, and **the pride of life, is not of the Father**, but is of the world. And the world passeth away, and the lust thereof: but he that doeth the will of God abideth for ever. 1 John 2:16-17"

> "Thefts, covetousness, wickedness, deceit, lasciviousness, an evil eye, blasphemy, **pride**, foolishness: All these evil things **come from within, and defile the man**. Mark 7:22-23"

The Father Honors The Son:

Being dedicated to using God's word. Increased my desire to give honor to the Father God, by honoring the words, and works of Christ.

I, was led to see by using the commands of the heavenly Father. I, see the work of Father God, always honors Christ Jesus, calling his Son, 'God'. And Christ vice versa honored his Father calling him, 'Father' and 'God'.

We see in the scripture, Christ Jesus, always honored his Father. And Christ commissioned us to honor the Father with our works. The same as we with works honor the Son Christ as Lord, and God.

> "That **all men should honour the Son, even as they honour the Father**. He that honoureth not the Son honoureth not the Father which hath sent him. John 5:23"

Kept In Focus:

In following the Lord Christ Jesus. It continually brings me back to what my focus is to be. In spite of the opinion, and choices of others. It is God's word directs me.

Keeping my mind focused on Christ, the living word, is a constant, and present help. Abiding in the presence of the Lord God, and his word, is preparation for me.

By being kept mindful, and focused on Christ. Allows me to face all situations. One of the blessed things for me in this life. Is recognizing true honor only comes from God:

> "I receive not honour from men. John 5:41"

> "For do I now persuade men, or God? or **do I seek to please men?** for **if I yet pleased men, I should not be the servant of Christ**. Galatians 1:10"

> "Jesus saith unto them, **My meat is to do the will of him that sent me, and to finish his work**. John 4:34"

Conflict Promotes Sharing:

By studying the life of Christ Jesus. I, became more accepting of the probability, of conflict. I, believe I, have felt hostility from some persons. Just because they are aware. That I, always seek to promote. The regular use of God's word.

Using the example, and commands of Christ Jesus. Using the word of God is my priority. Whenever I, am in the moment given the opportunity to minister. My efforts are all geared to give Christ the moment. To use me, in using his words

Seeking to please, and receive honor of mankind, is not for me. To avoid the use of God's words to please mankind is a 'no'. In serving God. I, do not avoid the use of God's word. Could never choice to have man's approval, over serving Christ.

As long as I, remain dedicated to following the LORD God. I, will hunger for God's Holy Spirit, inspired word. It is for making God's way known. That I, am fastened to Christ, and the use of God's doctrine.

Honoring God, by using God's word as he desires. Shall always have precedence over man's agenda. The major part of my ministry, is to prompt, all calling themselves Christians to follow, Christ Jesus as disciples:

> "Bind up the testimony, **seal the law among my disciples** Isaiah 8:16"

> "And he **stretched forth his hand toward his disciples**, and said, Behold my mother and my brethren! For **whosoever shall do the will of my Father which is in heaven,** the same is my brother, and sister, and mother. Matthew 12:49-50"

> "Then said Jesus to those Jews which believed on him, **If ye continue in my word, then are ye my disciples indeed;** John 8:31"

Cleave To God's Word:

We all need regular encouragement to adhere to Christ's words. And to Christ's word honoring example. We have before us Christ's commands for his disciples to observe and teach Christ's commission:

> "Go ye therefore, and **teach all nations**, baptizing them in the name of the Father, and of the Son, and of the Holy Ghost: **Teaching them to observe all things whatsoever I have commanded you:** and, lo, I am with you alway, even unto the end of the world. Amen. Matthew 28:19-20"

God's word from, the commands of Christ Jesus, are to be a daily life style practice. It is knowing Christ Jesus words are important to him. That daily encourages me, to follow the words. And the living practice of the Lord Christ Jesus.

Influence Not Easy:

It often is not easy to boost a thankful feeling in ministers. When they are enlightened that a doctrine they are spreading is not Christ's.

To show just by bible led teaching. That a doctrine, being spread in Christ's name. Is not what Christ Jesus lived, and taught. Is easily rejected with hostility.

It is by those in the long-time practice. Of spreading false doctrine that put up a great fight. Against Christ being the only true leader. Or the doctrine Christ said to teach, is the only truth.

It is always good to take a good look at any doctrine. When Mankind is leading mankind to follow. If a message is from the Lord God, it shall be speaking according to God's word:

> "For **he whom God hath sent speaketh the words of God**: for God giveth not the Spirit by measure unto him. John 3:34"

Directed By God's Will:

The effort itself, of helping others love the Lord Christ. Is to reveal Christ's purpose, from the scriptures. To hear Christ is the will of God. Christ's life was publicly lived, and his words were heard in public.

Christ's words, gave continual honor to his Father that sent him. The honor Christ gave to his Father was spoken openly, in public, and continually. Christ revealed that his purpose was to manifest his Father, so we would know truth, and live his love:

> "In this was **manifested the love of God toward us**, because that God sent his only begotten Son into the world, that we might live through him. 1 John 4:9"

> "No man hath seen God at any time; **the only begotten Son, which is in the bosom of the Father, he hath declared him.** John 1:18"

The reason I, recognize the purpose. For my seal by the Holy Spirit. Is that my life, by the Holy Spirit. Is enabled to testify of Christ. My actions, and words, are considered sealed.

Sealed to have, gracious words, and good works. To have righteous works, that testify of Christ, and give honor to God.

Prepared For Oppositions:

The reality of the importance, of trusting God's word. Gives me a steadfast, purpose. Benefiting from God's word, helps me to face difficulties.

My focus, to exalt the Lord God, and the word of God, shall continue to create, some hostility. But the Lord, gives joy in the midst of hostility. By the guidance of God's word. That has addressed hostility, and persecution.

By the experiences of Paul, and Silas we are able to identify how far persecution may go. I, rejoice in the record we have of those who acknowledged, and praised the Lord God. Due to being allowed to suffer persecution. Accusations by evil workers, with lies, shall always accompany the actions of persecution, to discourage righteousness:

> "And brought them to the magistrates, **saying, These men, being Jews, do exceedingly trouble our city**, And teach customs, which are not lawful for us to receive, neither

to observe, being Romans. **And the multitude rose up together against them**: and the magistrates rent off their clothes, and commanded to beat them… And at midnight **Paul and Silas prayed, and sang praises unto God**: and the prisoners heard them. Acts 16:20-22, 25"

Many Shall Not Accept:

Even though mankind is in desperate need of knowing, and following the Lord God. I, had to accept many shall not want to hear God's word. God's word taught me, many after hearing the word of God will not accept Christ:

> "And he said, **Take heed that ye be not deceived**: for many shall come in my name, saying, I am Christ; and the time draweth near: go ye not therefore after them. Luke 21:8"

The pride led, disobedient members of mankind. Will not feel the need for the light of God's word. The pride produced by sin, causes many to look for their acceptance. By the approval they want from mankind. And that is just the way it is, when taking time to consider the devil's part:

> "In whom **the god of this world hath blinded the minds of them which believe not**, lest the light of the glorious gospel of Christ, who is the image of God, should shine unto them. 2 Corinthians 4:4"

> "Enter ye in at the strait gate: for wide is the gate, and **broad is the way, that leadeth to destruction, and many there be which go in thereat:** Because strait is the gate,

and narrow is the way, which leadeth unto life, and few there be that find it. Matthew 7:13-14"

"How can ye believe, which **receive honour one of another, and seek not the honour that cometh from God only?** John 5:44"

"For **every one that doeth evil hateth the light, neither cometh to the light,** lest his deeds should be reproved. But he that doeth truth cometh to the light, that his deeds may be made manifest, that they are wrought in God. John 3:20-21"

Worth The Effort:

I, can say my, effort in honoring the word, of the Lord Christ Jesus. Is the blessing that prepares me for more blessings. Accepting the word, as the revealed truth of God. I can say without a doubt, I, have been building on truth to trust the one who is truth.

I, know my, word promoting, motivation, to exalt Christ. Is provided by the indwelling Holy Spirit. The presence of the Holy Spirit increases my desire. To search, and share the word. Because the main purpose of the Holy Spirit. Is to testify of Christ, and make his word known:

"But when **the Comforter** is come, whom I will send unto you from the Father, even **the Spirit of truth**, which proceedeth from the Father, he **shall testify of me**: John 15:26"

I, was given a strong desire from the word of God. As I remember how the Lord Christ Jesus, used the word. I, am committed in spite of objections.

To follow Christ, who promotes, and commands the living of God's word. Shall always have priority in my life. I, determined I, would search the scriptures.

To support the truth concerning life issues. As identified as truth from the word of God. Only what I, see was taught, preached and, lived by the Lord Christ Jesus, is used by me:

> "But though we, or an angel from heaven, preach any other gospel unto you than that which we have preached unto you, let him be accursed. As we said before, so say I now again, **If any man preach any other gospel** unto you than that ye have received, **let him be accursed.** Galatians 1:8-9"

> "But without faith it is impossible to please him: for he that cometh to God **must believe that he is, and that he is a rewarder of them that diligently seek him.** Hebrews 11:6"

> "For **we preach not ourselves**, but Christ Jesus the Lord; and ourselves your servants for Jesus' sake. 2 Corinthians 4:5"

> "According to the glorious gospel of the blessed God, which was committed to my trust. And **I thank Christ Jesus our Lord, who hath enabled me,** for that he counted me faithful, putting me into the ministry; 1 Timothy 1:11-12"

CHAPTER 5

KEEP SEEKING

The Lord Christ Jesus, has commanded us to keep seeking God's way, which in essence is daily following Christ Jesus. The primary reason why I see the Lord Christ was sent.

And has called for mankind to keep seeking, to search for truth. Truth is for there to be by us known, spoken, and followed. And there is noted growth from using the word. And dwelling in Christ for our soul's prosperity.

Christ the Lord, has made us aware of the need we have for new birth. Christ has revealed in his word. For us to be aware that we, must be born again. Is to me an illumination of our constant need.

To keep maturing in our daily progress towards Christ's kingdom, and his righteousness. We by the work of Christ with the Holy Spirit, are being sanctified.

Sanctification, I have learned from God's word. Is that by which we, by Christ's provisions. Are seeking, and progressing in our growth. To be by desire recipients, of the Lord Christ's righteousness. By growth in new birth. We are pursuing the privilege of imitating God's love:

> "Glory ye in his holy name: **let the heart of them rejoice that seek the LORD.** Seek **the LORD and his strength**, seek his face continually. 1Chronicles 16:10 -11"

> "If my people, which are called by my name, shall humble themselves, and pray, and **seek my face, and turn from their wicked ways**; then will I hear from heaven, and will forgive their sin, and will heal their land. 2 Chronicles 7:14"

The previous scripture, is one often used for giving strength, and encouragements. For strength in living what the love God requires. I, seek to have an abiding relationship with the Lord.

The prayer that is often used when we have prayer for our nation. I, find is beneficial good for individual use. The prayer used by nations is currently being used with sincerity.

It is by God's mercy that a nation is awakened. To it's need for the nation to seek to repent, and follow righteousness. We find in the scriptures, the appeal of all prophets. To serve the Lord God. With the love that responds, to living righteousness:

> "They **shall call the people** unto the mountain; **there they shall offer sacrifices of righteousness**: for they shall suck of the abundance of the seas, and of treasures hid in the sand. Deuteronomy 33:19"

> "And as **he reasoned of righteousness, temperance, and judgment to come**, Felix trembled, and answered, Go thy

way for this time; when I have a convenient season, I will call for thee. Acts 24:25"

Magnified Need For God:

I know the Lord God has used his word. To remind us we need him. By the inspiration of the Holy Spirit. The Lord has given, us. A constant reminder that, we need God. To mature by sanctification, into righteousness.

The Prayer prompting verse for the nations is the one, that prompts me to recall who the Lord is. The scripture verses that prompt the followers of the Lord God. Prompt them to go to him with all. The Lord's availability by his word, always comes to my mind.

In all things I find I have greatly benefitted from having the word. That invites me to acknowledge the Lord Christ Jesus is by his word leading to pursue life.

I find from God's word I am led to acknowledge, that Christ Jesus. Is the one who has laid in order the steps we are to take. There is no doubt, that the Lord God's purpose. Is for us to search, and use God's word, to live by. For our soul's to emerge into Christ's righteousness:

> "The righteous also shall hold on his way, and he **that hath clean hands shall be stronger and stronger.** Job 17:9"

The Word Must Be Lived:

In turning from evil ways, God word leads. God's way to redemption. The word must be followed. Christ Jesus in being our good shepherd, taught. What he preached, and taught must be lived, and taught.

The word of God the Father, was diligently followed and taught by Christ Jesus. As the word made flesh, for us to acknowledge, and follow:

> "**Whosoever therefore shall be ashamed of me and of my words** in this adulterous and sinful generation; **of him also shall the Son of man be ashamed, when he cometh** in the glory of his Father with the holy angels. Mark 8:38"

> "For I have not spoken of myself; but **the Father which sent me, he gave me a commandment**, what I should say, and what I should speak. John 12:49"

The ways taught, and lived by Christ Jesus, must be that, which is acknowledged first. When God's word says to seek his face, it is speaking to me of Christ Jesus' commands, and example:

> "For even hereunto were ye called: because Christ also suffered for us, **leaving us an example, that ye should follow his steps:** Who **did no sin**, neither was guile found in his mouth… Who his own self bare our sins in his own body on the tree, **that we, being dead to sins, should live unto righteousness**: by whose stripes ye were healed. 1 Peter 2:21-22, 24"

Christ Supports Love:

Christ Jesus the Lord's appeal for us to follow him, is reasonable. Christ's revealed purpose, and works, are supported, and motivated by the Father's love. By following Christ, in obedience we express love.

Christ seen as prophesied, is identified as loving the way of righteousness. The truth came by Christ's humble obedience to his Father. Christ in love, for righteousness sake, is able to fulfill all the needs of mankind.

I, started following fully after Christ when I, was led to hear Christ, and acknowledge God's word was being fulfilled in, and by Christ Jesus. I, came to recognize, my salvation need was not secure. By living the easy doctrine promoted by mankind.

I, recognized I, needed the Lord Christ Jesus. And I needed him to lead me every day. In order to achieve by his guidance, my need for new birth. I, rest in the assurance of having entrance into Christ's kingdom. By his constant and faithful leadership.

By acknowledging, and following the Lord Christ Jesus example, when contemplating any action. I, find I, am led by the word, and Holy Spirit. I choose the Lord's leading for positive direction:

> "**In all thy ways** acknowledge him, and he shall direct thy paths. Proverbs 3:6"

Constant Seeking:

I have learned the Lord God, has provided for me. to know him. Through various life experiences. I have learned even in familiar situations, I, need the Lord's leading.

From God's word, I, gained understanding, to know. It is for my best good, as spoken in God's word. For me to seek the Lord God in all my ways. I, recognize that I, need the Lord's wisdom for guidance.

I learned that I needed to be in God's word continually, with a constant attitude of seeking. I, learned I needed to have constant growth to fulfill my need, for my maturity:

> "Glory ye in his holy name: **let the heart of them rejoice that seek the Lord**. Seek the Lord and his strength, **seek his face continually**. 1 Chronicles 16:10-11"

Rest And Peace:

My rest, and peace comes to me. From learning the purpose of God's word. Learning the purpose of God's word. I gained more knowledge of Christ Jesus.

I, have from God's word also gained knowledge. Of the Father from Christ's life example. I, gain knowledge of how to get answers, for growth into righteousness. By remembering the words of Christ:

> "**If ye keep my commandments, ye shall abide in my love**; even as I have kept my Father's commandments, and abide in his love. John 15:10"

> "My son, if thou wilt receive my words, and **hide my commandments with thee; So that thou incline thine ear unto wisdom**, and **apply thine heart to understanding**; Proverbs 2:1-2"

No Questions Unanswered:

I, found questions commonly asked by mankind. God has answered them all. I, have experienced God as promised gives the answers.

God's needed faithfulness for comfort, is revealed, and present. In his unchanging word. Knowing God knows, and has answers to every situation, gives me blessed assurance.

By seeking the Lord God's view on every life situation, simple, and complex. I, find God's word of truth is proven reliable. All life situations are answered in the truth of God's word. Just as the Lord who abides in truth promised.

I, have found to achieve a life more abundant, it is expedient for me to stay upon God's word. The Lord has taught me, by seeking to continue my growth in knowing him, I, am seeing him better.

By abiding in the scriptures, and applying God's word daily. It is that which makes God's word enjoyable. It has afforded me enjoyable experiences. From seeking answers from God's word.

To be able to acknowledge the Lord, uses everything. As a source for revealing himself. Is itself, that which helps me, to grow in knowledge, and understanding of the Lord:

> "Hear, ye that are far off, what I have done; and, ye that are near, **acknowledge my might**. Isaiah 33:13"

Acting On What Christ Says:

In searching to know the Lord Christ, by going to his word. I have learned, the way, to know everything the Lord desires for me, is to know God's word.

I find in every difficult situation, there are promises from the Lord Christ. That gives me victory, by me believing the promises of the Lord:

> "In all thy ways **acknowledge him**, and he shall direct thy paths. Proverbs 3:6"

Finding the Lord in every situation, by his word. Is where I, feel the Lord's love is, and I am encouraged. I, am encouraged to fully embrace the Lord's constant unchanging truth. By finding that the Lord keeps his promises:

> "And ye shall seek me, and find me, when ye shall **search for me with all your heart**. Jeremiah 29:13"

> "Thy words were found, and I did eat them; and **thy word was unto me the joy and rejoicing of mine heart**: for I am called by thy name, O Lord God of hosts. Jeremiah 15:16"

Blessings In Bible History:

The main purpose the Lord God has given us in his word. Is for us to have encouragement. From the lives of those, who lived before us.

The most outstanding purpose. I have for going to the old testament. Is to gain knowledge of the Lord God. I see God for love sake making himself known, and how he works, in various ways being made known.

Cain A Blessed Lesson:

There is the case of Cain, receiving mercy (yes even the one who had murdered) Cain in his quandary after hearing what would accompany his error. Cain felt his need, and Cain felt his need could be met by approaching the Lord.

I think of how Cain had to realize he had a problem. And only God his Creator could give him relief from trouble. Cain recognized his need for mercy, and went to the one who is mercy:

> "**And Cain said unto the Lord, My punishment is greater than I can bear.** Behold, thou hast driven me out this day from the face of the earth; and from thy face shall I be hid; and I shall be a fugitive and a vagabond in the earth; and it shall come to pass, that every one that findeth me shall slay me.
>
> And the Lord said unto him, Therefore whosoever slayeth Cain, vengeance shall be taken on him sevenfold. **And the Lord set a mark upon Cain, lest any finding him should kill him.**
>
> And Cain went out from the presence of the Lord, and dwelt in the land of Nod, on the east of Eden. **And Cain knew his wife; and she conceived, and bare Enoch: and**

> **he built a city, and called the name of the city, after the name of his son,** Enoch. Genesis 4:13-17"

Remembering The Lord's Promises:

I think of Jacobs situation when he was about to face his angered brother Esau. The wronged brother Esau, was soon to face frightened Jacob.

It was against Esau, whom Jacob had by his mother's coaxing cooperated in deceiving his father Isaac to steal Esau's birthright, for self-gain.

It was by Jacob choosing his mother's advice that he took part in a scheme, to steal Esau's birthright. In a dire situation, Jacob realized in the presence of the fear of his past, God had come to him with promises.

By Jacob having remembered God being there for him. Jacob, took his concerns to God, and God's promises for him. Though Jacob was fearful of his brother Esau doing him harm.

Jacob remembering God's promises for himself, and his offspring. Jacob found comfort in knowing his future was in God's hands:

> "Deliver me, I pray thee, from the hand of my brother, from the hand of Esau: for I fear him, lest he will come and smite me, and the mother with the children. And **thou saidst, I will surely do thee good, and make thy seed as the sand of the sea, which cannot be numbered for multitude.** Genesis 32:11-12"

Different from Cain's appeal to the Lord for his own wellbeing, Jacob thought of the others, which could be affected because of his decision. Jacob appealed to the Lord, according to the Lord's promises to him.

The Lord God's promises to Jacob, included him, and his offspring being a great number. And the Lord God had also promised that Jacob, and his offspring would obtain good from the Lord.

God's Words Always To Be Remembered:

It was brought to my mind how Jacob's father Isaac, had appealed to God, for his wife Rebekah. At the time Rebekah, was barren, Isaac went to the Lord:

> "And Isaac intreated the Lord for his wife, because she was barren: and the Lord was intreated of him, and Rebekah his wife conceived. Genesis 25:21"

And we also have the view in God's word, of our Lord God's caring expressions of love towards individuals. When Rebekah had difficulty during her pregnancy, she approached the Lord, for herself, with her own concerns:

> "And the children struggled together within her; and she said, If it be so, why am I thus? And she went to enquire of the Lord. And the Lord said unto her, Two nations are in thy womb, And **two manner of people shall be separated from thy bowels; and the one people shall be stronger than the other people; and the elder shall serve the younger.** Genesis 25:22-23"

Rebekah's situation also taught me. How God loving variety, creates according to his will. I see how God is able to do in the womb of animal or mankind anything he desires.

Question Prompted By An Evangelist:

During a live streamed evangelical meeting hosted by a well-known, denominational-leader, evangelist Doug Baxler. In my spirit, I was led to seek God for an important answer.

By hearing comments Doug made, I was led to seek the Lord, for his answer. Because I had over time witnessed many ministers, from various denominations reporting. In the same manner as Doug Baxler.

It was at the end of the message that Doug made the statement, "no one knows what the mark of Cain is." It immediately came to my spirit, 'God knows':

> "And now art thou cursed from the earth, which hath opened her mouth to receive thy brother's blood from thy hand; **When thou tillest the ground, it shall not henceforth yield unto thee her strength; a fugitive and a vagabond shalt thou be in the earth**. And Cain said unto the Lord, My punishment is greater than I can bear.
>
> Behold, thou hast driven me out this day from the face of the earth; and from thy face shall I be hid; and I shall be a fugitive and a vagabond in the earth; and it shall come to pass, that every one that findeth me shall slay me. And the Lord said unto him,

> Therefore whosoever slayeth Cain, vengeance shall be taken on him sevenfold. **And the Lord set a mark upon Cain, lest any finding him should kill him.** And Cain went out from the presence of the Lord, and dwelt in the land of Nod, on the east of Eden. Genesis 4:11-16"

That very night after hearing the opinion Doug Baxler expressed, regarding Cain's mark. I prayed for the Lord to reveal to me the mark God had placed on Cain.

It was around 3am, three days after my prayer, when in my spirit I heard, "Mercy". After the word, "mercy", was emphasized to me, in my spirit. Several scripture verses came to mind, from Old, and New Testament.

The bible experiences, which were brought to my attention, gave acknowledgement to God's mercy. And with the confirmation of God's word. I gained a better understanding of how God's mercy follows us and answers our needs.

I, could see a very comforting message, because in Cain's distress. Cain went to the Lord God. How clearly it became evident to me, the same God invites us to go to him with all our concerns. The following scripture verses highlight, Mercy.

> "And he prayed unto the Lord, and said, I pray thee, O Lord, was not this my saying, when I was yet in my country? Therefore, I fled before unto Tarshish: for **I knew that thou art a gracious God, and merciful,** slow to anger, and of great kindness, and repentest thee of the evil. Jonah 4:2"

> "And David said unto Gad, I am in a great strait: let us fall now into the hand of the Lord; for **his mercies are great:** and let me not fall into the hand of man. 2 Samuel 24:14"

> "And when he heard that it was Jesus of Nazareth, he began to cry out, and say, Jesus, thou Son of David, **have mercy on me**. And many charged him that he should hold his peace: but he cried the more a great deal, Thou Son of David, **have mercy on me** Mark 10:47-48."

I appreciate so much the Lord's life teaching message on mercy, and the blessings that follows. I was led to consider how the mark of mercy from God, gave relief to Cain.

I see Cain settled down, with his wife. Cain had a son, which he named, Enoch. And being settled down, Cain built a city. And Cain named the city after his son.

I have been led to search the scriptures. I, am encouraged, by the availability of God's mercy. From the word of God, the following scripture verses illuminate. The need of all mankind, for the Lord God's mercy:

> "And the Lord passed by before him, and proclaimed, The Lord, The Lord God, **merciful and gracious, longsuffering, and abundant in goodness and truth**, Exodus 34:6"

> "(For the Lord **thy God is a merciful God**;) he will not forsake thee, neither destroy thee, nor forget the covenant of thy fathers which he sware unto them. Deuteronomy 4:31"

> "Thou **in thy mercy hast led forth the people** which thou hast redeemed: thou hast guided them in thy strength unto thy holy habitation. Exodus 15:13"

> "**Have mercy upon me,** O Lord; for I am weak: O Lord, heal me; for my bones are vexed. Psalms 6:2"

> "**Have mercy upon me,** O Lord; consider my trouble which I suffer of them that hate me, **thou that liftest me up** from the gates of death: Psalms 9:13"

Lesson From A Bird:

The lesson I learned from asking. A direct question of the Lord, concerning his work. I, learned the Lord encourages us. To go to him for all answers.

I, learned all the answers the Lord, provides gives hope. I have continued to ask the Lord questions, and I have at times received immediate response. For some questions, I have asked. I have received response a day or two later:

> "And it shall come to pass, **that before they call, I will answer; and while they are yet speaking, I will hear.** Isaiah 65:24"

There is the experience I had. With a red bird singing gleefully in our back yard. Finding I had no name for the red bird. I went to my husband, who was in the garage.

When I asked Bob, "what is the name of the red bird?" Bob did not know. It came to me as I was leaving the garage to ask God.

I went to God, with the same question. And immediately in my spirit I received the answer, 'Cardinal'.

Receiving the answer, I immediately turned back to the garage, and told my husband the name, and how I had asked God.

The experience I had with the cardinal, taught me to go to the Lord concerning all things.

I especially found I benefit more, by going to the Lord. And to seek his word concerning any matter. Even after, I have been given mankind's answer.

> "Blessed be God, which **hath not turned away my prayer**, nor his mercy from me. Psalms 66:20"

Expect The Lord's Presence:

For many years, I have had the Lord God's workings. Brought to my attention by memory of his word. The Lord, has blessed me, by revealing his ability. To keep me abiding in his abiding presence.

I have found, I, am encouraged, by people, situations, events, or objects, which are used by God. I, have illuminations, of the Lord God's ability, to keep himself known. By using all things, and using all events.

The Lord, wanting to be known. Remains easily approachable. And I, see the Lord God, as being worthy of praise. by working all things to make himself known.

I am by readiness from experiences. I'm reminded of, the Lord God's ability. I, have learned the Lord, fulfills all his soul comforting promises.

I, can testify as I, have seen the working of God. I, by ministering, find the reality of the Lord being always present, from the presence of God's word.

The word of God proclaims. God works all things, according to his established will. I, rejoice that all of God's promises, involves his Son's righteousness, and his faithfulness:

> "For **all the promises of God in him are yea**, and in him Amen, unto the glory of God by us. 2 Corinthians 1:20"

I find, there is no element, or creature that the, Lord God does not use to teach us about life issues. I, learn from observing various situations, and creatures. That, the Lord God stands true, in his, admonitions, and warnings:

> "Go to the ant, thou sluggard; **consider her ways, and be wise:** Proverbs 6:6"

> "It is better to go to the house of mourning, than to go to the house of feasting: for that is the end of all men; and **the living will lay it to his heart.** Ecclesiastes 7:2"

> "But **ask now the beasts, and they shall teach thee**; and the **fowls of the air**, and they **shall tell thee**: Or speak to the **earth, and it shall teach thee**: and the **fishes of the sea shall declare unto thee.** Who knoweth not in all these that the hand of the Lord hath wrought this? **In whose**

hand is the soul of every living thing, and the breath of all mankind. Job 12:7-10"

CHAPTER 6

Hope Filled Service

The experience of having that quiet voice speak within my spirit. Daily refreshes, my total being. The Lord God giving his Holy Spirit to be in me, and with me. Is the most persuasive evidence of the Lord God's word being true:

"And he said, **My presence shall go with thee**, and I will give thee rest. Exodus 33:14"

"**I will instruct thee and teach thee** in the way which thou shalt go: **I will guide thee** with mine eye. Psalms 32:8"

"And I will pray the Father, and **he shall give you another Comforter, that he may abide with you for ever;** Even the Spirit of truth; whom the world cannot receive, because it seeth him not, neither knoweth him: but ye know him; for he dwelleth with you, and shall be in you. John 14:16-17"

Special Ministry Promised:

The Lord God has allowed me, to enjoy him. Having knowledge of my activities. The experiences I have had, have convinced me. The Lord God's Spirit is active in leading. And does indeed dwell in me. To intervene, to encourage, and to correct me.

From the one special experience I, had. When the quiet voice speaking in my spirit. Encouraged me with the quiet, "I'm giving you a ministry".

Often when caught up in an activity. Of ministry that I saw was blessing people. I would think to myself, 'this is it'. I had been looking forward, to identify. What specifically would be my ministry. On which to give my full effort, and focus.

And to which I, was to wholly give my physical, mental, and spiritual energies towards. I would often conclude in my mind, that an activity was my ministry to focus, and build upon, in serving Christ.

I, often had that silent yet in my spirit audible voice. Repeating, "this is not it". I went through at least three, ministry events. That were filled with bible scripture sharing.

I, prepared bible bookmarks, and cards. Along with pocket calendars. I fully used. Every public, and ministry contact. To spread the gospel with tangible things to give-away.

I felt my aim was to provide something. Anywhere public exposure was available. And by me still seeking in my mind to claim the Lord's promise. That he was giving me a ministry. "This is not it". Is what I would hear from the Lord.

This Must Be It:

When I launched my first TV ministry, "See Jesus", on Public Access. I felt that was indeed my promised ministry. Due to the diverse public contact, that "See Jesus", afforded.

In my heart I felt assurance. I could settle it firmly in my mind. I, had been led by God, to my ministry. "See Jesus", was a pleasant, and an apparently needed program.

I was able to obtain contact, and feedback. From a broader range of viewers. Because, of all the subjects being offered. All were related to the Lord Christ Jesus. I, just knew it was surely the place. The Lord wanted my life effort.

I often communicated, the purpose. The program was, "to learn what the Lord Christ Jesus, is to us, and for us. Due to what was offered, I had assurance, 'See Jesus', was it.

Subjects, presented also, because of total communication. Attracted those wanting to learn ASL. There were teachers, students, parents, and grandparents, being encouraged.

Total communication, (sign language, along with speaking) provided me with opportunity. To reveal, and exalt the Lord, Christ Jesus. Because God's word, and songs were used to worship God. The program, was an asset for my growth and for the growth of many others.

Some whose purpose was to increase. In their desire to use ASL. Watched, 'See Jesus'. In order to pick up new signs, many watched.

Viewers, were also led to seek the Lord Jesus. For that, which he is. And for that which he does for mankind.

People of all walks of life, and even an Orthodox Jewish man. Gave me encouraging feedback. I, felt the feedback was confirming, 'See Jesus', was what God intended to be my lifetime focus for ministry.

I, could feel from the feedback. And the subjects presented I, was led to present. The TV program 'See Jesus' was greatly appreciated. And I could see, "See Jesus", Was. besides touching my life, it was touching lives.

Same as the prompting the Lord gave for me. To increase in his word. 'See Jesus' was God's avenue for my service. And maturity in growth. 'See Jesus', was without a doubt, touching lives.

"See Jesus", with sign language, allowed me. To present a steady focus on, the Lord Christ Jesus. The focus of the program. Allowed a full introduce of Christ Jesus. And to magnify Christ, through his symbolic roles.

In programs with such names as: 'See Jesus', 'Sent', 'Good Shepherd', 'Saving Health', 'God With Us', 'Our Light', 'Teacher'. And so much more. Many viewers along with myself, were enlightened. To the reality, of who Christ Jesus is, to us, and for us.

In over a hundred, and forty 'See Jesus' programs. Allowed more scripture sharing. Bible use supported prophesy support of subjects. 'See Jesus,' was presented twice weekly.

Christ was presented, as the, 'Holy One'. Specially emphasized was the truth. That Christ was sent was the Lord. As promised was purposely sent by his Father. With the same soul transforming love, of our Heavenly Father.

I, experienced that by me sharing on, See Jesus'. It was a blessing to capture, what his Father, and his mother Mary (by means of the Holy Spirit). Said concerning Christ. And what Christ, said about himself, and his purpose.

It was a precious encouragement to me. That God's word was constantly being used. To bless many participating, 'See Jesus' viewers. To fully accept, and worship Christ. Was the main purpose, I knew God had intended for me.

The following are some of the scriptures used on, 'See Jesus'. That are still magnifying who Christ is to us, and for us:

> "And there was a cloud that overshadowed them: **and a voice came out of the cloud, saying, This is my beloved Son: hear him.** Mark 9:7"

> "Jesus answered and said unto them, **This is the work of God, that ye believe on him whom he hath sent.** John 6:29"

> "The Spirit of the Lord is upon me, because he hath **anointed me to preach the gospel to the poor**; he hath sent me **to heal the brokenhearted, to preach deliverance to the captives,** and **recovering of sight to the blind, to set at liberty them that are bruised,** Luke 4:18"

> "Then said Jesus to them again, Peace be unto you: **as my Father hath sent me, even so send I you.** John 20:21"

Something so comforting to me, when I, truly accepted Christ Jesus. It was by learning how Christ lived, and taught righteousness.

In righteousness Christ humbly accepted the role of sin for man. The Lord accepted for man the unspeakable suffering by cruel treatment, and beatings. And then the cruel crucifixion. All suffering of Christ he endured in love. Because of the joy, that was set before him:

> "**Looking unto Jesus** the author and finisher of our faith; **who for the joy that was set before him endured the cross**, despising the shame, and is set down at the right hand of the throne of God. Hebrews 12:2"

Even A Child TV Ministry:

My husband Bob, just prior to, my TV production, had produced a TV program, which was viewed on Access TV, called, 'Even A Child'. I, had the pleasure, and blessing of being the Host, for 'Even a Child'.

And as it was shared by Steve, and Cindy Wright, when they shared their Marriage ministry on 'Even A Child', "the Lord God, in his spiritual, working is always present to behold".

My role, for, 'Even A Child', involved interviewing on TV, other Christ centered organizations. Bob did all the creative and technical work for, 'Even A Child'. And I, did the made the contacts, and did the interviewing.

Since I worked part-time Executive Assistant, at Family Life Radio. I, had the privilege of having contact with a variety of Christian ministries.

I was enabled by observation to become acquainted with. And select for contact, many ministries to interview on, 'Even A Child'. I also had access to persons. That were practicing ministers. Who also worked at, Family Life Radio.

Concerning the start of 'Even A Child'. The place where we then attended church as members. A church member, Charles Loadholt, was a TV producer.

Charles Loadholt, was needing help. For his program. "Life Style". Which aired on Access TV. Charles requested help with the cameras. Which required taking a training class, at Access.

An Open Door to 'Even A Child':

Bob, and I made an effort. To help Charles LoadHolt. By taking, the camera operating class. While present to take the camera class, (to assist Charles Loadholt). My, husband Bob, and I, were approached by a teenager TJ.

TJ, pretty much begged us. To take the Studio Production class. The Studio Production class, at the time. Was short by need of two people. TJ cane looking for two more participants. The class required putting in more time. And the enrollment fee, was a higher cost.

Bob and, I, signed up for the Studio Production class, which allowed us the opportunity to become producers. At the time we took the Studio Production Class. We were not planning to be producers.

Intro To Set Lighting:

Lighting, is the part of the Studio class. That really captured my attention. Lighting was the beginning. The most important instruction is lighting. Because the most important. Part of any production set, involves lighting.

The person teaching, I, don't believe was God fearing, But she gave to me a greater spiritual understanding. Of how the Lord of God, from Creation. Reveals who he is. And how God's soul strengthening principles. Are present in every life event:

> "**Thou hast beset me behind and before**, and laid thine hand upon me. Such knowledge is too wonderful for me; it is high, I cannot attain unto it. **Whither shall I go from thy spirit? or whither shall I flee from thy presence?** If I ascend up into heaven, thou art there: if I make my bed in hell, behold, thou art there. Even there shall thy hand lead me, and **thy right hand shall hold me.** If I say, Surely the darkness shall cover me; **even the night shall be light about me.** Psalms 139:5-11"

Just by giving information. On the importance of lighting. It really ministered. And continues to minister to me. The information on the purpose. And, importance of lighting inspired me.

To see Christ, as the true light needed for the set (to me life) and the work (gospel) of the Lord Christ Jesus. To be projected without distortions (lies, and conspiracies):

> "And God said, **Let there be light**: and there was light. Genesis 1:3"

The info I received from Studio Production class, regarding the lights affect, on the set. Was a great asset to me. Considering the set light, caused me to have a better understanding. Of the light of Christ, and his word on my life.

And there was a growing appreciation. Of the Lord Christ being presented in the word of God, as the true light. From my increased use of scripture. I, grew to appreciate, the one, whose life is the light of life, and who lights every man:

> "In him was life; and **the life was the light** of men. John 1:4"

> "That was the true **Light, which lighteth every man** that cometh into the world. John 1:9"

And my appreciation from God's word concerning light. Was from the truth of identifying. That all presented and claimed as being light by man. May indeed be an evil darkness:

> "But if thine eye be evil, thy whole body shall be full of darkness. **If therefore the light that is in thee be darkness, how great is that darkness**! Matthew 6:23"

The most important element on the stage is the lighting. Is in essence what was taught in the studio class. 'You can produce no light comparable to natural light. And natural light of Christ, is the best. By which we are to create.

We were directed to see how bad lighting. Could distort, and darken the image. You are trying to illuminate. 'Even A Child', was created by Bob in the year 2000. To share the Lord's working in different ministries. And how he lights different lives.

Today from the experience of interviewing many diverse, and willing ministries. With their focus on serving, the Lord God. I can say in essence, 'it's all about the Lord'. It's all about the Lord,' was often my closing statement. As I hosted, 'Even A Child'.

The Lord gave me an acrostic for the title. Even though the bible scripture with the name was good. The Lord, enabled me to use, each letter of the verse. To represent God's desired work. In giving the everlasting gospel. In all of the world's nations:

> "Proverbs 20:11 Even a child is **known by his doings**, whether his work be pure, and whether it be right."

Every Voice Every Nation All Carry His Indwelling Light Daily:
E V E N A C H I L D

Acknowledging The Lord:

The acrostic is an example of how. The Lord God showed me. He is involved in everything. And it inspired me to use the acrostic. On a badge I, created during public appearances.

To emphasize the Lord's purpose. For the program Bob produced. As I recall the many organizations, I had the pleasure of interviewing. I learn from, and rejoice in the Lord. For being who he says he is. And doing what he does.

I, can appreciate so much more. The Lord God, always providing for our effort. For his namesake, and our Heavenly Father's glory:

> "He **restoreth** my soul: he **leadeth** me in the **paths of righteousness** for his name's sake. Psalm 23:3"

> "But when it pleased God, who separated me from my mother's womb, and **called me** by his grace, **To reveal his Son** in me, **that I might preach him** among the heathen; immediately I conferred not with flesh and blood: Galatians 1:15-16"

I realize how it caused me. To better see the Lord's purpose, for me. Which was to emphasize the Lord Christ Jesus. By the Lord Jesus being presented.

I, could see, scripture clearly taught. The only Son was sent. To be the head, and to command obedience. To live following his righteous example. And support his planned authority.

To be the promoter of truth. And bow to the one that is. Elected by his Father to lead his church. All the way into his righteous kingdom.

In every opportunity of ministry. I began to share. and emphasize. How Christ Jesus is revealed, as the one. For mankind to know to follow.

Christ Jesus, is the one we are to serve. And how we are to focus. On exalting Christ only. In place of other agendas:

> "For **we preach not ourselves**, but Christ Jesus the Lord; and ourselves your servants for Jesus' sake. **For God, who commanded the light to shine** out of darkness, **hath shined** in our hearts, **to give the light** of the knowledge of the glory **of God in the face of Jesus Christ.** 2 Corinthians 4:5-6"

First 'Even A Child' Broadcast:

We started the first program, and TV interview on, 'Even A Child', with Carl Jackson. Who at the time, was a minister. Working at Family life Radio. Carl, and his wife Anna who prayed for, 'Even A Child' to succeed. In ministering for the Lord.

During my interview, Carl Jackson, used time well. In emphasizing how mankind needs. To have a relationship with Christ. "We strengthen each other, by speaking the word."

Carl Jackson, by regular practice, used God's word devotedly. During the TV presentation on, 'Even A Child', Carl Jackson, and, I, freely discussed what it meant, to be one in Christ Jesus.

The person, and work of, the Lord Christ Jesus was freely discussed. Sharing the gospel message. Was a blest, part of our first program.

'Even A Child' TV broadcast, was soul fulfilling. I was blessed with a feeling of joy. From recognizing, the privilege, 'Even A Child' allowed ministries to share. And it blessed the viewers that expressed their gain from tuning in:

> "**Thou hast made known to me** the ways of life; **thou shalt make me full of joy** with thy countenance. Acts 2:28"

Payoff From A Request:

One of the remarkable things that happened. Following our first program showing. At a time, we were setting up in the studio for another interview. We, were approached by several youth led by TJ.

TJ walked in with other youth that asked the question, "did TJ get you started?" And we answered, "yes". I remembered the smiling appreciative face of TJ, that appeared relieved.

The youth TJ gained relief, from our thoughtful. Which was the truth because it could not be denied. The Lord did use TJ's need. To get our TV ministry started. I recognized, TJ's expression of relief. We could have said, 'no'.

Due to knowing the one. Who really used TJ, to get us started. Maybe we should have shared, with the youth. .That it was the will of God, who used TJ. To accomplish God's purpose.

Bob's Creativity Paid Off:

It was obvious that TJ, also had a reason. For boasting to his friends. Concerning, 'Even A Child'. Bob had created, what anyone could appreciate. Many described the set as being, 'a real cool intro'. It was a catchy intro to 'Even A Child' program.

'Collegic' was the identification. One of the head officials at Access. Gave Bob's creation. Bob used carefully chosen music. And some visual entities swirling around.

The program's cool intro included me. Seated on a ladder beside a large studio camera. The music, and visual creation, in itself. Announced, this was a very special program.

Offered A Gift:

Bob's creation really caught the eye, and the ear. Which excited the youth, and also, some not so young. There was an engineer named, Andrew, who gave us a very complimentary offer.

Andrew's offer involved him. Wanting to use his skills and equipment. To design, and construct for, 'Even A Child'. A fold away special TV setting, as a gift.

It was a great encouragement for Bob, and I. To recognize the impact the program had, due to a special offer, graciously made by Andrew to us.

The engineer Andrew, expressed his view of the value of the program. Though Andrew had considered himself, a Christian all his life. Andrew mentioned, he had learned some new, and good things.

My Special And First Shared Message:

The pomegranate as the gospel fruit, was the icon used, for 'Even A Child'. And it was a revelation given to me spiritually. And was the first time I, used the gospel fruit lesson.

Identifying those sealed by the Holy Spirit, after hearing the gospel, and the roles they were assigned. It was the Lord who gave me spiritual eyes to see the meaning of every part of the pomegranate.

Theme Song Inspired Action:

'Even A Child's theme song, was the words, sung by Matt Redman, stating, "Many are the words we speak, and many are the songs we sing, but now to live the life".

Bob by thoughtfully searching, was led, to the song, which stirred an accountability, challenge. The challenge of the song Bob chose, was for self, and others.

To walk the spiritual talk. And to talk the walk, by living it. In essence, the word says, to live according to Christ. The living light, and word of truth:

> "But **be ye doers of the word, and not hearers only,** deceiving your own selves. James 1:22"

Song "Now To Live The Life":

> "Many are the words we speak Many are the songs we sing Many kinds of offerings But now to live the life x2 Help us live the life x2 All we want to do is bring you something real. Bring You something true (We hope that) Precious are the words we speak (We pray that) Precious are the songs we sing Precious all these offerings But now to live the life, Help us live the life x2 All we want to do is bring you something real Bring You something true x2. Now to go the extra mile Now to turn the other cheek And to serve You with a life Let us share your fellowship Even of your sufferings Never let the passion die...Now to live the life..."

The song Bob picked, by Matt Redman, offered the prompting to identify more fully. What the Lord Christ Jesus, for love's sake requires. The son, song Bob, chose. Captured the very purpose for following Christ. For what our, daily living should be speaking. In our worship of the Lord.

The words of the theme song. Used to start off every program. Encouraged viewers, and really encouraged Bod, and I. We were encouraged to recognize we, were purposed for the Lord God's glory. And not for uplifting, and broadcasting ourselves, not for self-recognition.

I, especially have received encouragement. To lift up the Lord Christ Jesus. Who in the manifested love of the Father. And is presented all through the scripture. As our, 'Rock', to build our, lives upon.

The Lord Christ is mankind's. Only God given path to Salvation. Who by love was sent as promised, to remove sin. And by Christ the abominations of sin. Are exposed, to be removed from us. I, rejoice for every opportunity. To say, all that mankind needs. Is provided by Christ the Lord. In response to his Fathers, love:

> "Know ye that the **Lord he is God: it is he that hath made us, and not we ourselves;** we are his people, and the sheep of his pasture. Psalm 100:3"

> "Only fear the Lord, and **serve him in truth with all your heart**: for consider how great things he hath done for you. 1 Samuel 12:24"

"My soul, wait thou only upon God; for my expectation is from him He only is my rock and my salvation: he is my defence; I shall not be moved. **In God is my salvation and my glory: the rock of my strength, and my refuge, is in God**. Psalm 62:5-7"

Opportunity For Ministry:

For 12 years 'Even A Child', presented ministries that had the reputation for serving God. 'Operation Blessing'. 'Operation compassion Blessing' with Jim, and Sue Wingate, followed Carl Jackson, which shared the upcoming, 'Festival Of Hope'.

"Festival Of Hope', provided words of hope, with service to mankind action. 'Festival Of Hope' emphasized compassion, which Christ Jesus, lived, preached, and by example, taught.

'Festival Of Hope', presented on 'Even A Child', was the time when Christians of different churches, were seen. Actively serving in any way they were able. To highlight the many that were approached. And got out of the pews, to show, and receive compassion.

Every type of need that, is prominent in our society. It could be identified, were being served. We interviewed those, that were offering care. And the care administered. By diverse ministries, was seen on 'Even A Child'.

Ministries which gave scripture answers, and principles dealing with Marriage, began with, 'Marriage Missions'.

'Marriage Missions', with Steve, and Cindy Wright.

Steve, and Cindy shared the features of a healthy marriage, related to Christ, and his Church. It was shared how commitment, to the relationship with Christ, helps marriages grow and last.

The, 'Covenant Family Counseling Center', with Tim Smith, a devoted Christian counselor. Tim's devotion to Christ led him besides using psychology to refer to bible scriptures.

Tim used the principles found in God's word, in helping those who sought, his counseling, guidance. Tim was also readily open, to assist anyone who had a family related problem.

Tim, though a Christian, foremost was there, to serve all persons with needs. Without recommending that they accept Christ Jesus, if they were not inclined:

> "But I say unto you which hear, **Love your enemies, do good to them** which hate you, Luke 6:27"

> "And when he had called unto him his twelve disciples, **he gave them power against unclean spirits, to cast them out, and to heal all manner of sickness and all manner of disease.** Matthew 10:1"

Tim acknowledged the Lord Jesus made mankind whole. And Jesus delt with physical, mental, psychological, and relational ills. And for that reason, Tim served all avenues.

What I, especially appreciated from Tim. He stated his confidence was in the Holy Spirit. Always being present to give him needed guidance:

"Howbeit **when he, the Spirit of truth, is come, he will guide you into all truth:** for he shall not speak of himself; but whatsoever he shall hear, that shall he speak: and he will shew you things to come. John 16:13"

Word Sharing Opportunities:

Attending the 'Festival Of hope', allowed, 'Even A Child', to prepare programs. Bob would video tape me interviewing ministries at the festivals. From the interviews of ministries serving needs with compassion. Programs were made.

The ministries of, 'Operation Blessings', and 'Festival Of Hope', gave the grateful opportunity, for me, to carry bookmarks. To share my bible verse, bookmarks, and bible verse pocket calendars.

Making Christ Jesus known as the head of his church. Was a determination, which became precious, and motivated me. As ministries were interviewed I, shared. The purpose given by Christ. I began to also realize. All our efforts were all about Christ Jesus:

Bookmarks, with a variety, of diverse scripture verses became a powerful tool in serving, the Lord God. Bible verse cards, became a well received, opportunity. For me to share the word of God. I was able to see God work in some up-close, and personal ways.

The tangible gift, of the varied scripture inscribed, items added a positive close encounter with individuals. Giving away bible verse inscribed, bookmarks. Also gave recipients the opportunity to receive randomly selected bookmarks.

I, was especially blessed when a person would share with me, that one of the bookmarks I gave them (usually from three) answered their current concern.

I Created scripture book marks, that went with me to share everywhere. The Lord God, has blessed me, to have the remembrance, of the way created book marks. Touched lives near, and far. I, would also leave a variety of bible bookmarks at any church, which, we would attend.

Interest And Knowledge Revealed:

My most memorable experiences. With the spreading of God's word, using bible bookmarks. Happened I, was while working. From my desk, as I worked part-time at Family Life Radio.

I could observe, persons entering, and leaving the front office.

On one occasion, as I sat at my desk, I observed a mother carrying a book, and her teenage daughter, enter the front office. It was immediately that, I had in my spirit the prompting, to 'give her three book marks'.

I took time with selecting three bookmarks. And as I opened my office door. While extending the bookmarks to the mother. I made the statement, 'the Lord wants you to have these'. As I gave the bookmarks to the mother.

There was a look of shock on the face of the daughter. And glee on the face of the mother. Referring to her daughter the mother stated, 'she had just said to me, you don't even have a bookmark for your book'.

The mother disclosed in laughter, how she had been using a torn piece of paper as her marker. And her daughter was teasing her over the matter.

I have often been led to praise God. For his impromptu caring appearance. Even in making himself known, in small matters. Which enabled me to have. Impromptu moments of rejoicing in the Lord.

Something so simple as the need for a bookmark, God used to help all present, (a mother and daughter, Diane office Sec., and myself) to see God's love, and more of his caring. And also, from time to time, the Lord, reveals his sense of humor.

A Friend Encounter:

Margarita Real, a radio station visitor. Who also became a friend, who also took on sharing my bookmarks. As part of her ministry.

Margarita's husband (a gun enthusiast), frequently attended gun shows. And, Margarita went with him, carrying bookmarks. Gun show attendance, gave opportunity to Margarita. As she accompanied her husband.

And it became an outstanding opportunity for Margarita to share bible verse bookmarks, near, and far. I was led shortly before I, met Margarita. To create bible verse, bookmarks, in English, and in Spanish. Which was beneficial to Margarita, who shared both, in diverse places.

Margarita with a gentle manner. Came into my life with a concern. Wanting a relationship with the Lord, Margarita shared with me, 'I don't really feel I have a relationship with the Lord'.

Margarita was my second up close. Opportunity to share, the Holy Spirit. I remember with enthusiasm. Sharing from scripture the Holy Spirit. I, shared the sealing, and the work of the Holy Spirit, with Margarita.

And I remember Margarita. Responded with the same joy, I had. The help of the Holy Spirit was growing. God provided a much needed, and live assistant. For the much needed work of believers.

Margarita allowing me to share. With her the good news of the, Holy Spirit. Gave both of us the opportunity. For actively sharing God's word. Margarita I, remember gaining. Comfort in the Lord, from accepting. The work of the Holy Spirit.

My new friend became interested. And actively shared the bible bookmarks. The bible bookmarks went everywhere Margarita went. As she accompanied her husband, to gun shows.

Margarita even distributed bible bookmarks to a person with a gun related business. Who also by contact with me, received some of my email devotions.

The most encouraging bookmark distribution involved a lady, I'll call Ester, a devoted lover of Christ Jesus. A Catholic lady of Peru, noted to have a passion for Christ.

Time for Ester to go home. Ester, made a request for bookmarks, to go home with her. I, prepared in Spanish, a large boot size box of laminated bookmarks. To go home to Peru with Ester.

When I, made bookmarks in large numbers. To be sent to other countries, which happened occasionally. The one valuable thing the Lord taught me. Was to just keep moving in the direction. Which I use for accomplishing a variety of interests. I, became proficient in multitasking.

God's word, by Margarita, was sent to places out of state. After nine-eleven, at a time I was giving out bookmarks. As I gave a bookmark to a news-camera-man. Who was present at a 'Hope Feast' with a large camera.

In my mind I still picture the camera-man, looking with concentration at the book mark. The image on the bookmark was of firemen lifting the flag. And at the time the thought came to me. That New York, was one of the places Margarita had been sending bible bookmarks.

'Even A Child', Door Opener For Others:

It was our 3rd program when Mickey Grace, an especially appreciated Radio Announcer. Mickey being by birth a Jewish man. It thrilled listeners to hear Mickey share Christ.

I know now it was a challenge for Mickey Grace. When working at the radio station. To share the music of Messianic Jews. And whenever Mickey under some restraint. Would share music intended for Jews, and Gentiles.

The blessings and appreciation for Messianic music. Would be communicated by some Christian listeners. Mickey Grace's involvement in Christian ministry. Would reveal to me there was in the Christian community. Some hostility in the Christian church community, towards Jews.

I, wonder If there shall ever be full acceptance. By the church community, for Jews in Christ. I found many in the church community carry, and spread a hostility. Derived from not willing to accept Jews, as being in Christ.

Mickey's appeal during his presence on, 'Even A Child', was to encourage viewers to explore. The power of God's word. Jewish people were specifically. Encouraged to read God's word.

Mickey Grace allowed me to gain. Knowledge of the growth of. Of the Messianic Jewish congregations. And to gain a whole hearted. Appreciate for God's timing.

There was a Messianic Jewish ministry on radio, which I contacted to give the opportunity to share on TV, but they declined, 'we're not ready yet'. I, did however, become friends with the wife Heidi, a 4th generation Jewish believer in Christ Yeshua.

Though Heidi, could not okay her husband's work to be shared on, 'Even A Child', Heidi, and I became friends. I gathered ministry, blessings from Heidi, in reports. And pictures Heidi shared. Which allowed me to enjoy the Jews, and Arab peoples, oneness in Christ. By Christ's mercy I, was blessed by Heidi's influence.

Knowing Heidi's experiences in Jerusalem. Demonstrated to me Christ's love, and favor, for Jews and Arabs. And how by both Jews and Arabs knowing Christ.

Christ creates relationships between Jews, and Arabs. That are promoted, and blessed by love. I also learned how more Jews with Arabs were believers. A worshipping Christ blessing. Shared on my other produced, and Hosted program, 'Come Children'.

Even A Child Sharing Continued:

Many episodes later #25 that, we had the opportunity, to present, 'Brian Richards, Public Baptism'. 'Even A Child' was there and involvement at the baptism event of. 'Full Gospel Business Men'.

One of the business men, Bob Sedor (serving the homeless) encouraged, effort to baptize the homeless. Bob Sedor was known to make the appeal to the church community, "Don't just feed them, baptize them."

It was during the period of time, when the public baptism was happening. That the effort of individual church members came to light.

The Start Of "One In Messiah":

One of those baptizing, at the public baptism. Was, a Jewish congregational leader, Steve Shermet. The congregational leader Steve Shermet, was of Beth Sar Shalom (House Of The Prince Of Peace).

We took the opportunity to introduce, 'Even A Child' to Steve Shermet, and arranged. To present BSS on Bob's TV program. After first presenting, Beth Sar Shalom. We started attending BSS.

Attending Beth Sar Shalom. The Messianic congregation. Became a learning place for us. And 'Even A Child' gave BSS, an open-door for outreach.

After airing BSS on, 'Even A Child', there was positive response. Viewers started to connect with. And some attended BSS with interest, and enthusiasm.

After a time of regularly presenting, BSS on 'Even A Child'. Bob encouraged Steve, to purchase a camera, and have BSS members. For ministry purposes, get trained at Access. To operate worship capturing cameras.

It was not long after receiving a camera. And the training of a few BSS, members. That there was a name, and a song that was selected "One In Messiah". The TV ministry program,

'One In Messiah' was presented on Access. And it continued to grow members, Jews, and non-Jews, worshipping 'Yeshua', together.

Pastor Otis Brown Jr. was the 7th ministry we shared. Due to favorable accounts, from fellow Ministers. I contacted Pastor Otis Brown Jr.

At the time of, Pastor Otis Brown Jr's, ministry sharing. He had an on-going, and active, 'Cell' ministry program. Pastor Otis Brown Jr shared. The operation of his churches cell program. Emphasizing that it followed. The pattern Christ gave. By having twelve disciples,

It was emphasized, by Pastor Otis Brown. How Christ Jesus started with twelve members. That grew into other small groups. Small groups that kept growing.

Pastor Otis Brown Jr, shared how the intention of sharing the gospel. Was being achieved by small groups. From encouraging small groups of his members. Some small groups, were reaching out from homes. And were reaching out to non-members.

Some interviewed members, of Pastor Otis Brown Jr's cell groups. Were enthusiastic by the results of their effort. In reaching out. Many were encouraged to participate. And there was noted growth, in small groups. Knowledge of salvation, was being enhanced. By small group participation.

One of the outstanding events, concerning Pastor Brown's community involvement. Was that, of being chosen by pastors. To head the 2001, New Year service. The service involved multicultural. And multidenominational participants.

Pastor Otis Brown Jr, and his efforts caused Bob to have respect for him. And Pastor Brown was given the opportunity, to share, 'Siloam Freewill Church'.

Bob provided assistance and a start for allowing Pastor Otis Brown, to have his own TV ministry. Which is still presented from present church, now named 'Siloam Christian Church.'

Bob in honoring the Lord. Did many things very well, by using his skills. To benefit the spiritual growth of others:

It is a pleasure to identify the ministries helped by Bob to have TV outreach. Which are still being blessed. And continues to be shared. Through various media streaming means.

'Come Children'

I was also inspired to produce another TV ministry program. Which, gave the opportunity for sharing Christ, and the word of God in a variety of creative ways.

The TV ministry program that I produced shortly after, 'See Jesus' started a 30 min program, which immediately went to 58 min. 'Come Children' was a program I, planned to have something for children of all ages. Which I presented on Public Access for a little over 13yrs.

By the time it ended (due to decrease of City funding), 'Come Children' rendered blessings with every showing. I can freely testify of seeing God's purpose. To have his word to be made known, being fulfilled.

I truly felt the Lord's guidance. From the start, to the Program's conclusion. And I can even say, after the program ended. I still have feedback from those who benefitted from the messages presented on, 'Come Children'. And I, had requests to restart the program again.

Presentations chosen for, 'Come Children', told me I was not alone in my selection of the titles. The order of the themes in the presentation. Leaves me in the state of thanking Jesus. And I, grew spiritually in the content, And from the bible verses, Pictures, videoclips, and songs chosen.

I still rejoice over the opportunity. The remembrance of God's encouraging guidance. Still keeps me looking to him. Since

I, am still feeling from feedback. The enthusiasm the Lord's delight afforded.

'Come Children', a twice weekly program, allowed each episode to be televised twice. The program, 'Come Children', had eight ministry, sections, up to the time of, 'Come Children's conclusion.

Sections of, 'Come Children', and order shared: 1. The Word, (the Son, the beginning, true light) 2. The Holy Spirit (works with word, baptizes, Seals, teaches) 3. Sing To The Lord (offer direct praise) 4. Salt And Light (disciples, witnessers for Christ, stewards) 5. Life Lessons (used items and events to teach) 6. Being Healthy (for body, heart/mind, do what the word says) 7. Bible Rondo (used word, music, rhythm, stress oneness in Christ) 8. Know Our Enemy (expose Satan's purpose and work, God's plan, God's armor).

The title that I gave, to a program's episode. Was based on the 'Life Lesson', that was being presented. I chose to use the 'Life Lesson' title, because. It gave a spiritual lesson. And it usually spoke, to a current life event, need, or pleasure.

Few subject titles of, 'Come Children', program episodes were, 'After It's Kind, 'Seed Within', 'Knowing The Way'. And 'Dying', in which I, shared my Mom's passing. Just before my Mom's spirit returned to the Lord.

The fulfillment I gained from producing, 'Come Children'. I realized I, had, an up-close relationship with the Lord. Spiritual growth, in myself. And that was communicated. By viewers for self or family members. It became a lasting joy, as it was evident. I was ministering, to myself. As I, blessed the Lord in ministering to others.

Just knowing what I was led, to produce. Was serving the Lord. Gave me satisfaction. With every program effort. By serving the Lord, I was given the pleasure. Of seeing progress, from every episode of 'Come Children'.

In ministering to the lives of others. From my devoted service to the Lord. I, started growing more. Into the increased need of God's word.

The Word Set The Stage:

The 'Word' section always allowed the opportunity to use God's word in a variety of ways.

The most blessed use of the word. Was in presenting the Lord Jesus as the one the Father gave. Full authority in providing salvation.

And the appreciation of the Lord. For Christ's humble submission to take on. The physical likeness of mankind. Which allowed us kinship. I am led to recall there was an increase in faith.

As the identity of Christ (the word). Was shared with all, 'Come Children,' program. Was noted to be affecting, all ages. And all spiritual needs.

Recognizing the need to emphasize. The Lord God's work. The word of God was to be highlighted first. The word became the life stirring element. Of each presented program. Considering God's word first, became, a necessary practice. During any life sharing, consideration.

Pointed out during, the section on, 'Word'. The word was how God, started everything. The word had the forefront. Of everything, that the Lord God did. Presenting special features of God's word. Controlled the start, for all my, 'Come Children', presentations.

Emphasis was on how the word of God. Was to come above, any effort of mankind. Was, and is my focus, and delight. Presenting God's word first. Set the value of God's word. To be considered, before all things.

The need to know, and follow God's word. Was often stressed to the viewers. And I, often had the pleasure of meeting viewers. And conversing with some of the viewers.

I, am still blessed to know, God also selects the persons needing him. And God, allowed me, to meet grateful viewers. It still gives me great pleasure.

As I, realize the past and my, experience. With spiritual darkness, I, am blessed. By being able to note how God has shown up. And has blessed the past experience. Of a dark spiritual place, that I, moved through.

I have from the Lord his pleasure. That has led me, to treasure. That I, am treasured. And equipped to provide. God's word focused worship: The truth of the good news, is that God is the beginning.

We, have the record that Christ, is. The light, from the beginning. And that Christ, is the word that keeps us in his, light, of truth.

From the beginning Christ, as appointed by his, Father. Gives, the ceaseless light of life, and truth:

> "**In the beginning God** created the heaven and the earth. Genesis 1:1"

> "**In the beginning** was the Word, and **the Word was with God,** and the **Word was God**. John 1:1-2"

> "**In him** was life; and **the life was the light of men.** John 1:4"

> "That was **the true Light**, which lighteth every man that cometh into the world. John 1:9"

> "And **God said, Let there be light**: and there was light. Genesis 1:3"

To me God saying let there be light. Was the Father saying, 'Son take your rightful place. May we endeavor, to keep the Son of God. In his rightful place. For ourselves, and for the other persons, God, loves:

> "**And God said,** Let there be a firmament in the midst of the waters, and let it divide the waters from the waters. And God made the firmament, and divided the waters which were under the firmament from the waters which were above the firmament: **and it was so**. Genesis 1:6-7"

Life Purpose:

To strengthen the life focus of viewers. The need for being in God's word daily. Was constantly, and strongly encouraged. Following is the main verse used. To emphasized the need of God's word in presenting. The need to have knowledge of Christ:

> "O earth, earth, earth, **hear the word of the Lord**. Jeremiah 22:29"

And I, used a scripture that gave emphasis. To why the word of truth. Had to be heard and trusted. Before Christ could be trusted, and believed. And why the word had to be heard. And why to be sealed, by the Holy Spirit. Christ as the word. Had to be believed.

In order to truly accept Christ. The Old Testament scriptures that proclaim Christ. Is to be accepted, as Christ taught. The importance of the word of God.

Being first in giving the knowledge of Christ. The good-news is expressed in the following verse. This scripture verse is a special one. I learned to treasure. As soon as I, heard It:

> "In whom **ye also trusted**, after that **ye heard the word of truth**, the gospel of your salvation: in whom also **after that ye believed, ye were sealed** with that **holy Spirit of promise**, Ephesians 1:13"

The Holy Spirit:

'The Holy Spirit', was the section, of 'Come Children', that acknowledged the needed work, and Godhead position of the Holy Spirit. The fruit, and gifts of the Holy Spirit. Were highlighted in word, and song. For their life enhancing, provisions.

The video used for the start, and finish of, 'Holy Spirit,' section, was a dove descending downward, and then moving upward. The purpose, to identify, the work, of the Holy Spirit. That allows all believers to grow, in following, Christ.

In the section, of the Holy Spirit. There was emphasis, for believers. To see themselves moving, towards Christ. By the work, of the Holy Spirit. We start to exalt Christ. Same as the Holy Spirit. And, we achieve Soul transformation.

For gain of the Spirit's fruit. And the gifts, of the Spirit. For exalting, and testifying. Of Christ Jesus. And to know how, the Holy Spirit. Enables new-birth. By using the word of God.

The conclusive message I emphasized. Was the importance of knowing, 'if we don't have the Holy Spirit, we do not have Christ,':

> "But ye are not in the flesh, but in the Spirit, if so be that *the* Spirit of God dwell in you. Now **if any man have not the Spirit of Christ, he is none of his** Romans 8:9."

> "But when the Comforter is come, whom I will send unto you from the Father, even **the Spirit of truth, which proceedeth from the Father, he shall testify of me**: John 15:26"

I witnessed more growth in myself. From following, Christ's words. Concerning the work of the Holy Spirit. The enlightenment, I, received. from hearing. The word concerning the Spirit. And I believe keeps increasing. My growth. From the evidence of my, experience.

Because I was in my, spirit strengthened. In seeing the Lord's purpose. And the Lord's promises, being fulfilled. I sought to promote the importance. Of having the Holy Spirit:

> "But the Comforter, which is the **Holy Ghost**, whom the Father will send in my name, he **shall teach you all things, and bring all things to your remembrance**, whatsoever I have said unto you. John 14:26"

> "But when the **Comforter** is come, whom I will send unto you from the Father, even the **Spirit of truth**, which proceedeth from the Father, **he shall testify of me**: John 15:26"

Sing To The Lord:

'Sing To The Lord', was a section of 'Come Children', which encouraged knowing, the Lord God. Influenced by the Lord's praise evoking plea. The Lord gave the blessing.

By the use of, many of his servants, voices. Used to sing to him, and of him. For stirring, and elevate, His excellence. And to delight. In his works of wonder.

'Sing To The Lord', was to me a healthy release. And it focused on the importance. Of taking time to praise God. 'Sing To The Lord'. Provided a thought, provoking time. For giving full recognition, to the Lord God. To proclaim the I, am, he, is. And what from the description of self, he, does.

Consideration to who the Lord God is. And what the Godhead (Father, Son, and Holy Spirit) does. Was enabled by magnifying. The Lord God's worthiness. Presented in songs that were in content purposeful. And the songs, were in what they offered. An expression of my, love to the Lord.

'Sing To The Lord' was especially created. To inspire the program viewers. To sing to the Lord a new song. New songs from varied artists were shared.

The songs, with the word of God. Encouraged viewers, to the word, with songs. Some bible verses that were used. Before a song was shared. Were the following scriptures:

"I will praise the name of God with a song, and will magnify him with thanksgiving. Psalms 69:30"

"O sing unto the Lord a new song; for he hath done marvellous things: his right hand, and his holy arm, hath gotten him the victory. Psalms 98:1"

"Praise ye the Lord. Sing unto the Lord a new song, and his praise in the congregation of saints. Psalms 149:1"

"Speaking to yourselves in psalms and hymns and spiritual songs, singing and making melody in your heart to the Lord; Ephesians 5:19"

"Let the word of Christ dwell in you richly in all wisdom; teaching and admonishing one another in psalms and hymns and spiritual songs, singing with grace in *your hearts to the Lord* Colossians 3:16."

Songs from various music ministers, were such as, "There Is None Like You", "I Love You Lord", "Your Love Never Fails", and "Salvation Is Your Name"

Salt And Light:

'Salt And Light', was the section that gave full attention. To the purpose of being called the, body of Christ. And what it meant to be commissioned. To serve Christ Jesus. And the heavenly Father. A closing emphasis was that. What Christ said was to be sought, and followed first:

> "But **seek ye first the kingdom of God**, and **his righteousness**; and all these things shall be added unto you. Matthew 6:33"

A chosen introductory video for 'Salt And Light'. Would have word's that emphasized our role. As the body, and servants of Christ. The light of the world. Mentioned in the section. At different times. Was that, we are salt, the essence of good. In the world by being, Christ's.

The light of the world. Fishers of men. Witnesses, stewards, etc. According to what Christ said. Concerning our roles would be shared:

> "**Ye are the salt of the earth**: but if the salt have lost his savour, wherewith shall it be salted? it is thenceforth good for nothing, but to be cast out, and to be trodden under foot of men. Matthew 5:13"

"**Ye are the light of the world**. A city that is set on an hill **cannot be hid**. Matthew 5:14"

"**Let your light so shine** before men, that they may see your good works, and **glorify your Father** which is in heaven. Matthew 5:16"

"And he saith unto them, **Follow me**, and **I will make you** fishers of men. Matthew 4:19"

"My sheep **hear my voice,** and I know them, and they **follow me**: John 10:27"

Blessing Of Considering Who:

The most important focus. I had pleasure from considering, and sharing. Is the 'who' of Christ Jesus. That Christ the Lord, is the Great, Everlasting, True, and Marvelous Light. He gives me, eyes of understanding. To see Christ way through, and in the dark.

I was led to see because, I, belong. To the Lord Christ Jesus, (my, true light). By his word, and Holy Spirit of light. He leads me, in truth. Given in scripture, to inspire us.

I, benefit from the bible record. Of servants, of God, and those not servants. From the Old Testament. And from the New Testament. And it keeps me from confusion. And blesses my life. To see God's, faithfulness. In his word, adds to life.

To give light from our lives. By pointing by words, and actions. To the Lord, is emphasized. It was, and is with great pleasure. for me. To have contentment in emphasizing truth.

We are led to be blessed. By observing the Lord's work in lives. Especially in observing the lives. Of those, who, from the beginning. Trusted in Christ, from the. Prophesies, given of Christ.

In Christ it was emphasized. We are to be known by a reputation. In speaking, and doing good works. And we are blessed by the desire. To live in like manner, as Christ. As the faithful followers of the Lord. Who were before us. Devoted, to God. And devoted to following. God's word.

In taking note of the faithful believers. That trusted in, and had hope in Christ. I, find it is beneficial to share. The description, of the characteristics. Of, some of the servants of Christ. That in faithfulness, went before us.

Daniel:

> "I have even heard of thee, that the spirit of the gods is in thee, and that **light and understanding** and **excellent wisdom** is found in thee. Daniel 5:14"

Peter And John:

> "Now when they **saw the boldness** of Peter and John, and perceived that they were **unlearned and ignorant** men, they marvelled; and they **took knowledge of them, that they had been with Jesus.** Acts 4:13"

I found in acknowledging. The leading of Christ as the light, for my life. Opened my eyes to my purpose. Acknowledging Christ as my Lord. Led me to be active. In doing all I can. to consider Christ's leading. In every life situation. Through, and in the dark:

> "Then spake Jesus again unto them, saying, **I am the light of the world:** he that followeth me shall **not walk in darkness**, but shall **have the light of life.** John 8:12"

> "As long as I am in the world, I am the light of the world. John 9:5"

> "I am come a light into the world, that **whosoever believeth on me should not abide in darkness.** John 12:46"

When it comes to being salt. Considering the qualities of salt, is a blessing. When taking into consideration. The Lord, provides a variety of salts. In a variety of characteristics, and strengths. I, learned to appreciate. The Lord being a consuming fire. Is the one that gives the zeal. For serving the Lord:

> "For **every one shall be salted with fire**, and every sacrifice shall be salted with salt. Salt is good: but if the salt have lost his saltness, wherewith will ye season it? Have salt in yourselves, and have peace one with another. Mark 9:49-50"

> "Let your speech be alway **with grace, seasoned with salt**, that ye may know how ye ought to answer every man. Colossians 4:6"

Life Lessons:

'Life lessons' was the section. That allowed me to explore. And share lessons from life. It was a pleasure for me. To share the many ways God, teaches every day. With life objects, creatures. And my, life experiences:

My, most memorable, lessons. Were those, that were happened. Upon, natural, and immediate. Life objects, and experiences. The light, pomegranate, eggs, seed pods. And creatures, of every description.

The blessing of the 'life lessons' God's, word had priority.

To promote, and share. Specific ways, of the Lord Jesus. It allowed me to give encouragement. For viewers. To seek, and look for the revelations, of God. In, the things God created. Things we use in daily life. And reports from world events.

Being Healthy:

'Being Healthy', started with a video, of a potter's hands working the clay, into the form of a pot. My, key statement used often in that section was, 'To be healthy in body, heart, mind, and spirit, is to know what God's word says, and follow it.'

'Being Healthy', gave me the opportunity. To search God's word, for what. God requires of mankind, for health. It was a pleasure to share.

Much of the knowledge I, shared. Was from what, I, had gained from education. And from working, in care giving capacities. Involving, nursing. And social service considerations.

This section encouraged me. To share the serious influence. That can direct, the practice and behavior. In all areas of the soul. And have a lasting impact on a person's life. I was encouraged to zero in on. The Lord God's love, and his over-all purpose. To, bless us with good health.

In the section on 'Being Healthy' There was emphasis on how. Each part of our being. Is to compliment the other parts. Body, heart/mind, and spirit. Were highlighted, as the parts. To be considered, and respected. As part of 'the soul,' the man.

Helping persons identify. One part cannot be, well or sick. And not affect the other parts. To understand, that all our parts. Are connected. And any part neglected. Takes away from the other parts. The sincere striving for health. Of each part, was encouraged.

Bible Rondo:

This section of the program. Most viewers I had contact with. Identified the section, as being, their favorite. 'Bible Rondo'. provided the welcomed opportunity. To be exposed, chanting and rhythm experiences.

I had a father's letter, telling me. His then 4-month-old, baby girl, was alert, and joyful. All during the time 'Bible Rondo', which she. Looked forward to, and watched. At the start I, would chant in rhythm, 'Bi-ble Ron-do'.

Following the drum beat. I would speak with the beat drum, and the instrumental, 'Across The View by, Richard Burmer. Following are the words I spoke, at the start of 'Bible Rondo':

> "We are all in a circle that goes all around the world, and everyone in this circle, has accepted the Lord Christ Jesus. Yet there is still room for others, to join-in. Jesus is the center of our circle, and he draws all of us, to have love for one another."

After I had ended the starting words of, 'Bible Rondo', I, with the drum would beat out a chosen bible verse, and then go into the message of the verse chosen.

I had viewers share with me. How the bible rondos, led them to become aware of many good. And unknown to them, scripture verses.

And there were reports, of 'Bible Rondo'. Helping individuals, in remembering scripture verses. The father of the 4-month-old. Shared that he, was moved by Psalm 27:1, which is also one of my, favorite. Life in Christ, edifying, and life comforting, verses.

The rhythmic comforts of Psalm 27:1. I, used, with the beating of the drum. The following pattern: "The Lord-is- my light-and my-sal-va-tion-whom -shall I fear?–the Lord–is-the strength -of my life;–of whom-shall I-be afraid?"

The very start at the beginning of a, 'Come Children', started with a video showing children in various activities with the children's voices heard singing the words, 'Come into the holy, of holies, worship at the throne of grace x3, and then ending with, 'Jesus, Jesus'.

The words of the song were also used at the entrance of 'Bible Rondo', but just the part, 'Come into the holy of holies, worship at the throne of God'.

'Bible Rondo' I enjoyed very much. Because, it allowed me to freely. Explore and sharing. Many bible, subjects. And my greatest of all pleasures. Was to know growth in God's word. Was being achieved by many others. The ending of 'Bible Rondo'. Was concluded by a song. Praising the word of God.

The song portion I believe I enjoyed using most was, 'Thy word is a lamp unto, my feet, and a light unto my path", and occasionally I, would use the song, "The B-I-B-L-E".

Know Our Enemy:

'Know Our Enemy'. This section, began, with an illustrated view of a coiled snake. A resemblance of an evil angel, and a roaring lion. Along with the illustrations. Were related scriptures read by, Alexander Scourby.

The verses read by Alexander Scourby. Were from the books of Genesis, Isaiah, Ezekiel, and Revelation. To give insight into, Lucifer. The covering cherub who chose evil. After his heart became lifted up. Leading Lucifer, to become, Satan. The devil, the serpent, the dragon, and more. And contributed to, the world's evolving darkness:

> "Now **the serpent was more subtil** than any beast of the field which the Lord God had made. And **he said unto the woman, Yea, hath God said,** Ye shall not eat of every tree of the garden? Genesis 3:1"

> "And **the serpent said** unto the woman, **Ye shall not surely die**: Genesis 3:4"

> "**How art thou fallen** from heaven, **O Lucifer**, son of the morning! how art thou cut down to the ground, **which didst weaken the nations!**

> For thou **hast said in thine heart,** I will ascend into heaven, **I will exalt my throne** above the stars of God: **I will** sit also

upon the mount of the congregation, in the sides of the north: **I will ascend above** the heights of the clouds; **I will be like the most High.**

Yet thou shalt be brought down to hell, to the sides of the pit. They that see thee shall narrowly look upon thee, and consider thee, saying,

Is this the man that **made the earth to tremble, that did shake kingdoms;** That made the world as a wilderness, and destroyed the cities thereof; that opened not the house of his prisoners? Isaiah 14:12-17"

"**Thine heart was lifted up** because of thy beauty, **thou hast corrupted thy wisdom** by reason of thy brightness: I will cast thee to the ground, I will lay thee before kings, that they may behold thee.

Thou **hast defiled thy sanctuaries by the multitude of thine iniquities,** by the iniquity of thy traffick; therefore will I bring forth a fire from the midst of thee, it shall devour thee, and **I will bring thee to ashes upon the earth** in the sight of all them that behold thee. All they that know thee among the people shall be astonished at thee: thou **shalt be a terror, and never shalt thou be any more.** Ezekiel 28:17-19"

"And **there was war in heaven**: Michael and his angels fought against the dragon; and the dragon fought and his angels, And prevailed not; **neither was their place found any more in heaven.** And the great dragon was cast out, that old serpent, called the Devil, and Satan, which deceiveth the whole world: **he was cast out into the earth, and his angels were cast out with him.** Revelation 12:7-9"

"Be sober, be vigilant; because your adversary **the devil, as a roaring lion, walketh about, seeking whom he may devour**: 1 Peter 5:8"

The purpose of 'Know Our Enemy'. Was to clearly identify. The characteristics. And the actions of the devil. To show there is a definite. and noted difference between. The identity, and lie promoting works of Satan. In opposition to God's identity, as love. And the righteous works of God.

The blessing I had from serving, the Lord. In presenting the section on, 'Know Our Enemy'. At the time I, realized the Christian churches, were not. Mentioning the devil, and his tricks. Many saying they were Christians, were denying, and dismissing, the devil's power.

Many teach, the devil cannot touch their lives. Because they are Christians. I learned in presenting the section, 'Know Our Enemy'. To have the viewers consider. What Christ experienced. And what Christ said, concerning the devil.

Ministry To My Mom:

Years before my mom passed away, except for the last couple of years of my mom's life. My mom spent time in three different Long Term Care facilities.

Since I was trained, and took part in active holistic, care rendering services. By being regularly present I, recognized various deficits involved in the care facilities.

Seeing written, and spoken promises of care not being carried out, besides some indications from my mom, I, became convinced the regular presence of loved ones was necessary.

The word's the Lord provided in the scriptures regarding needed care promised but not being fulfilled, came through to me, loud, and clear. There is a simple but true revelation in God's word, of why needed care is not provided:

> "But he that is **an hireling, and not the shepherd, whose own the sheep are not, seeth the wolf** coming, and **leaveth the sheep, and fleeth**: and the wolf catcheth them, and scattereth the sheep. The hireling **fleeth, because he is an hireling, and careth not for the sheep.** John10:12-13"

I, see the wolf being any need not met. And with there, also being many persons, needing to work, being unprepared bad things happens.

Many persons are put into positions without proper training. A fact I, found to be true from my, observation, and which is a known concern expressed by all persons, who have experience with care facilities:

> "Also, that the soul be **without knowledge, it is not good**... Proverbs 19:2"

To benefit my mom, I had the privilege to daily, provide active quality time in assisting her. Due to seeing the need, I played a major role in my mom's much needed over-all care.

The word's the Lord provided in the scriptures regarding caring for parents came through, loud, and clear to me:

> **"Honour thy father and thy mother**: that thy days may be long upon the land which the Lord thy God giveth thee. Exodus 20:12"

> "Hearken unto thy father that begat thee, and **despise not thy mother when she is old**. Proverbs 23:22"

From my holistic training, I was able to see needs, my, mom had. And I, responded to my, mom's needs, by helping my mom meet her needs.

My mom's needs included; obtaining appropriate meals, bathing, maintaining cleanliness, toileting, and special grooming.

Having my mom involved in activities, that would contribute to, her over all well-being, was the purpose of my presence. An issue, important to both myself, and my mom, was proper nourishment.

One of the main events I enjoyed with my mom, was seeking the facilities, provisions to be provided for my mom. It was my mom's delight to be included in entertainment, and worship events.

Group activities allowed my mom, a time to be active in expressing her uniqueness in participation. I, made sure when weekly church activities were held, my mom was properly dressed, and well groomed.

I, would arrive at the facility to assure my mom, to meet her desire had the opportunity to worship. And I enjoyed worshipping with my mom.

Worship Participation Top Priority:

There was a noted rejoicing of my mom, during the time assistance was provided, for my mom, to attend church. Church attendance allowed my, mom to dress special, and congregate with others.

My mom was special in lifting her voice in praising God. And hearing God's word, was always a blessing, to my mom. In order, for my mom, to fully enjoy singing. I, typed all the songs and I, made a laminated hymnal for my mom.

Making the laminated hymnal for my mom, contributed to my mom enjoying the worship space of time more. Meeting my mom's need it allowed one of the residents, who had trouble with the size of the regular hymnal print, to communicate her visual problem.

For the resident, who communicated her problem, I, responded. It was also a delight to my mom that I, provided a laminated large-print, hymnal, to meet the visual need of another person. I am blessed this very minute by how time with the Lord, and a loved one blesses so much:

> "Lord, I have loved the habitation of thy house, and the place where thine honour dwelleth. Psalms 26:8"

> "Surely goodness and mercy shall follow me all the days of my life: and I will dwell in the house of the Lord for ever. Psalms 23:6"

Early Life Training Remained:

Worshiping the Lord, I, can see, was a life comforting experience, which my mom, carried with her from her youth. My, mom, was from the family that often traveled to minister.

And one of my mom's grandmama's sisters was a Pastor, along, with her husband. My older sister, and I, had the privilege of visiting, the Pastor aunt of my mom, and we were humbly ministered to, continually.

I, had the experience of walking into a facility, and find my mom, with her head bowed, eyes closed praying. I, also had the blessed experience, of walking in, and finding, my mom, praying for other persons that were living at the facility.

The experiences I, had with my mom, reinforced the blessings, I, have received concerning training a child. And I, now more than ever seek to encourage parents to put out all effort, for the souls of themselves, and for their children:

> "Train up a child in the way he should go: and when he is old, he will not depart from it. Proverbs 22:6"

> "Those that be planted in the house of the Lord shall flourish in the courts of our God. They shall still bring forth fruit in old age; they shall be fat and flourishing; To

shew that the Lord is upright: he is my rock, and there is no unrighteousness in him. Psalms 92:13-15"

"And all thy children shall be taught of the Lord; and great shall be the peace of thy children. Isaiah 54:13"

"Train up a child in the way he should go: and when he is old, he will not depart from it. Proverbs 22:6"

Door Opened For Me To Bless:

"I, can still hear the question being asked of me, by Delores one of the main Methodist church ministry leaders, 'could you help us?' I, never sought to find out if they were aware of my, TV ministries. But that still small voice, had already given me, the thumbs up that I, was going to be ministering to the residents there.

My mom's expression, on her face was that of pure joy. As she took part in worship under, my leadership. The message, with the planned accompaniments of worship order, and specific songs, were mine to choose. As I served the residents, and attending staff the Lord, ministered in a special way to my mom, and to myself.

Why We Worship God:

I, remember the first message, which I, gave at the facility, which followed the song, 'Holy, Holy, Holy'. I, started my, first message with the question, 'why do we, worship God?'

At the moment, I took my position up front, my mom smiled with approval, and apparent pride. To my question, many had puzzled expressions, and one of the wise residents responded, 'because he is God'. And to build interest in my message, I, asked, 'what makes him God?'

Getting into the Lord, as Creator of all things, and worthy of praise, honor, and glory, proved to be the right start for my first message, at the LTC facility.

My first message opened the door to keep the focus of my other messages to give full attention to our God. I, stayed strongly planted on the majesty of the Lord God, and his worthiness.

I, was blessed from the opportunity I, was given to serve the Lord, God in the facility. I was blessed by having full control of the service contents, which caused me to depend more upon the Lord God's leading.

It turned out I served in ministering at the facility by providing approximately thirty messages. One of my most memorable, messages was an acrostic on, loving God.

My message was, in essence, we love the Lord God, by **Looking** to him, in all our ways:

> "Hebrews 12:2 Looking unto Jesus the author and finisher of our faith; who for the joy that was set before him endured the cross, despising the shame, and is set down at the right hand of the throne of God."
>
> "Proverbs 3:6 In all thy ways acknowledge him, and he shall direct thy paths."

We love him, by **O**beying him:

> "Jesus answered and said unto him, If a man love me, he will keep my words: and my Father will love him, and we will come unto him, and make our abode with him. John 14:23"

We love God by **V**oicing his words:

> "For he whom God hath sent speaketh the words of God: for God giveth not the Spirit by measure unto him. John 3:34

And we love God, by **E**xalting him:

> Lord, thou art my God; I will exalt thee, I will praise thy name; for thou hast done wonderful things; thy counsels of old are faithfulness and truth. "Isaiah 25:1 O"

The experience the Lord allowed me in that facility gave me opportunity, for growth. Every experience of my seeking to bless the life of my mom, and others, gave me the opportunity, to become better acquainted with the Lord God.

There was also the Lord's continual presence to enlighten me, to the reality of mankind's response to truth. I, was reminded that truth, offends, and often offends individuals, because of their offensive anti-truth practices.

On one occasion I noticed the facility had a calendar, which carried a theme for the month. I started using the facilities, monthly theme in giving my message, which turned out to offend the facility when, 'Client's Right's was their theme.

Using a few scripture verses, I gave the definition of rights, and how Christ is our perfect example of how to treat people with dignity. The following scripture verse was used, to show the Lord God's leading in providing, 'Client Right's':

> "But the wisdom that is from above is **first pure**, then **peaceable, gentle**, and **easy to be intreated, full of mercy and good fruits, without partiality, and without hypocrisy**. James 3:17"

In emphasizing the example of Christ. I, was led to capture, the instructions. Demonstrated, in the life of Christ. And Christ's teaching, and preaching massage. On loving him, by meeting the needs of others.

The work of Christ, I, must say answers my many questions, concerning, what part does caring for others have in defeating sin. Christ's main messages for love's sake are all geared to meeting the needs of fallen mankind.

The Lord Christ gives to us. The life, saving command. To know him, and follow him. It is by the word of God. That I, see, God's, fast of his choosing. Is to humble self, in giving love to him, and others.

The best fast I, found to take. Was to cease fully from my, vain thoughts, and my, works. To give my, attention. To fully know, and follow, the God's way (which is Christ):

> "Is not this the fast that I have chosen? to loose the bands of wickedness, to undo the heavy burdens, and to let the oppressed go free, and that ye break every yoke?

Is it not to deal thy bread to the hungry, and that thou bring the poor that are cast out to thy house? when thou seest the naked, that thou cover him; and that thou hide not thyself from thine own flesh?

Then shall thy light break forth as the morning, and thine health shall spring forth speedily: and thy righteousness shall go before thee; the glory of the Lord shall be thy rereward. Isaiah 58:6-8"

"He hath shewed thee, O man, what is good; and what doth the Lord require of thee, but to do justly, and to love mercy, and to walk humbly with thy God? Micah 6:8"

CHAPTER 7

HOPEFUL STILL

The many blessings I, have received. Are from all the experiences, I, have encountered. I can say the Lord, has fully taught me about ministering.

By the way the Lord God. Has ministered to me, I have grown. I am blessed by recognizing. I, shall always need the Lord God. And the Lord never stops ministering to me.

More ministry experiences, has placed before me, the Lord's provided opportunity, for me, to consider the way the Lord God leads. I, have by seeking, learned to consider my approach to ministry, by the way, the Lord is daily leading me.

More and more, I have accepted the importance of growing in the knowledge of Christ's life lived message. I, now know, I need to see more of Christ imparted, to every message I hear concerning, who the Lord God is, and his will for us.

I, now cherish the importance of knowing, it is, a great pleasure to give the utmost glory, and honor to the Lord God. A most important message, and necessary consideration, confronts all members of mankind.

Top of mankind's question list, I, find is, 'who is God, and what does the Lord God, require of me? In general, the answer of who, the Lord God is, and what he requires of mankind, are questions, to which many answers are given.

Many answers that are given concerning God, are given by false prophets. All we need to know concerning the Lord God's desire for us, is in his word.

The reason why, the Lord Christ Jesus, told those hearing him to live by every word of God is for safety. The written, and living word, is our only defense against the deceitfulness of sin.:

> "Thus saith the Lord, the Holy One of Israel, and his Maker, Ask me of things to come concerning my sons, and concerning the work of my hands command ye me.
>
> I have made the earth, and created man upon it: I, even my hands, have stretched out the heavens, and all their host have I commanded.
>
> I have raised him up in righteousness, and I will direct all his ways: he shall build my city, and he shall let go my captives, not for price nor reward, saith the Lord of hosts. Isaiah 45:11-13"

In my, commitment to serve the Lord God, I, become acquainted with the fact that the Lord leads by various means. I found in every area, and experience, I have had was, and is a teaching event, which allows, my acquaintance with the Lord God's ways to take place.

In every area of ministry, even impromptu, situations, I find the Lord God, has been faithful. So important to me is finding the Lord God is faithful in keeping the promises given in his word.

In searching God's word, I see, in every way, the Lord fulfills, his promises. Being dedicated to the Lord God is where, I, see the Lord is always leading, me to be. I, realize the Lord has given me a sacred opportunity, to willfully humble myself to be fitted to serve him.

Anytime a situation comes about, I, find there is mental, and spiritual growth in taking the time, to consider, from scripture, what the Lord, has to say.

I, now fully realize it is a most precious, and sacred opportunity to learn from the Lord Christ's word's and life. From Christ, we receive the answer in full concerning who the true God I to, and for us.

I, have learned to seek to keep a willing, and obedient spirit in growing in the Lord God's grace, which sanctifies. I, believe to follow the Lord Christ, according to his word, is to me, to accumulate priceless, treasure:

> "If ye be willing and obedient, ye shall eat the good of the land: Isaiah 1:19"

Accumulating Treasure:

I, know I, am accumulating treasure in my earthen vessel, as I keep seeking, to know the Lord God. I know as I, keep growing by searching, asking, and knocking, as the Lord God leads me, I shall at the same time be serving him.

The Lord Christ, and his heavenly Father's leading is the way for me to remain restored, in the Lord God's righteousness, which gives me his peace. To know the Lord God is leading me, and by following the Lord God, he leads me, to seek, ask, and to knock.

Concerning the gain of knowledge, understanding, and the wisdom the Lord God requires for me to have, I go to the Lord God's word. Knowing the Lord's desire, and requirements for me, is also a sacred treasure.

Knowing, the Lord Christ Jesus, is forever my soul restoring shepherd, gives peace to my soul. As I, abide in Christ, and seek to follow him, every day, makes my life worth living:

> "He maketh me to lie down in green pastures: he leadeth me beside the still waters. He restoreth my soul: he leadeth me in the paths of righteousness for his name's sake. Psalms 23:2-3"

> "But rise, and stand upon thy feet: for **I have appeared unto thee for this purpose, to make thee a minister and a witness** both of these things which thou hast seen, and of those things in the which I will appear unto thee; Acts 26:16"

The Lord My Ministry:

The Lord is ready, and able to complete his work in all believing members of mankind. The Lord asks that I, recognize I, am his, and I, have his victory, as I, submit to him.

The most comforting, and blessed truth, I, have experienced is that the LORD, works as he said. I, especially rejoice to claim, the LORD God, works in me, and through me.

By the Lord God, abiding in me, and me, abiding in him. I, experience that I, am being ministered to, for my growth in my appointed ministry.

The Lord Christ, gave clarity as to my calling, by repeatedly revealing what my, work would look like. Christ emphasized God's word, is to guide mankind's life.

By depending also upon his Holy Spirit to lead me. I, look for all goodness, righteousness, and truth within myself, as I, submit my weakness to the Lord:

> "And he said unto me, My **grace is sufficient for thee: for my strength is made perfect in weakness**. Most gladly therefore will I rather glory in my infirmities, **that the power of Christ may rest upon me.** 2 Corinthians 12:9"

> "Humble yourselves in the sight of the Lord, and **he shall lift you up.** James 4:10"

> "Wherefore **he is able** also to save them to the uttermost that come unto God by him, seeing he ever liveth to make intercession for them. Hebrews 7:25"

By knowing from experience that the Lord, keeps his promise, to guide me in all my ways, I depend upon him. By being submitted in all my ways before the Lord God, I, minister for the Lord's glory.

My steadfast effort, to know, and please the Lord, I recognize is due to the works of God within me. I see my efforts themselves, minister to the Lord God, who first ministered to me.

The Lord God is the one who, by his word approached me to seek to know the Lord. Seeking to know the Lord Christ Jesus, and the heavenly Father, I was led to apply diligence to my searching God's word by subject.

My searching to fully know the Lord God leads me, by the Lord God's desire.

The Lord God's desire for me, leads me to want to know what the Lord God requires of me. As I, seek God's will I, find he speaks to me at any given moment.

Most assuredly, I, have grown by the blessing, of knowing the answer to all questions, is in God's word. And as planned is seen in the life of Christ Jesus:

> "**He hath shewed thee**, O man, what is good; and what doth the Lord require of thee, but to **do justly**, and to **love mercy**, and to **walk humbly** with thy God? Micah 6:8"

Direction From The Lord:

In all of my efforts in all my ways, I look to the Lord. And for all of my efforts, the Lord, is constant in teaching me.

It is the Lord God, by his provisions, who instructs, and provides. The Lord provides me, with experiences, which allows me to see, and trust in him.

Keeping my focus on the life of the Lord Christ Jesus, is that which promotes my efforts. Knowing the Lord Christ Jesus, by what he commanded, and lived, drives the passion of my efforts.

It is by seeking to stay in fellowship with the Lord Christ Jesus, that constantly teaches me, and guides my efforts. Any time, I, have identified persons or organizations not growing, is where I, see, the Lord Christ Jesus, is not exalted, and honored as leader.

The place where the Lord Christ Jesus, is not whole-heartedly followed, is where truth is lacking. I, recognize the habit of rejecting, or not seeking God's word do not have a relationship with Christ. Those that reject God's word, refuse the Lord Christ Jesus', leadership. And have no desire to make the Lord God known.

There is no effort by man, to follow the Lord God, when Christ's life example is ignored. Christ Jesus' life example, gives me comfort, as I realize, the Heavenly Father has spoken clearly to the world, through his Son's life.

I, can see Christ Jesus lived the message he tells us to observe, and share with the world. Having an attitude led by Christ's Holy

Spirit, is the only position, I find comfort in seeking, establishing, and maintaining:

> "Thus saith the Lord, **Stand ye in the ways, and see, and ask for the old paths,** where is the good way, **and walk therein, and ye shall find rest for your souls.** But they said, We will not walk therein. Jeremiah 6:16"

> "Give unto the Lord the glory due unto his name; worship the Lord **in the beauty of holiness.** Psalms 29:2"

Knowledge Of God Required:

From the beginning of mankind's time on the earth. The Lord God has provided mankind. With the opportunity to know him. Growing in knowing the Lord, leads me, to giving, the Lord God, (Father, Son, and Holy Spirit) glory, and honor:

> "Thus saith the Lord, Let not the wise man glory in his wisdom, neither let the mighty man glory in his might, let not the rich man glory in his riches: But **let him that glorieth glory in this**, that he **understandeth and knoweth me,** that I am the Lord **which exercise lovingkindness, judgment, and righteousness, in the earth**: for in these things I delight, saith the Lord. Jeremiah 9:23-24"

> "But of him are ye in **Christ Jesus, who of God is made unto us wisdom, and righteousness, and sanctification, and redemption:** That, according as it is written, He that glorieth, let him glory in the Lord. 1 Corinthians 1:30"

"Whether therefore ye eat, or drink, or **whatsoever ye do, do all to the glory of God.** 1 Corinthians 10:31"

Christ Over-all:

The Lord God in his word, has led me to see. All the way from Genesis, the everlasting gospel points to Christ Jesus, our salvation.

We, arise by the work of Christ Jesus, from the difficulties evolved from the result of sin. And it is in Christ the Lord, that I, find I have full access to Christ's triumphant victories every day.

All that represents the will of God the Father is seen in Christ. The Lord God's ways for us, are identified, and obtained through the Lord Christ Jesus. God's way I, find can be fully seen through the knowledge, and the ways of the Lord Christ Jesus.

I, am fully Led, to overcome undesirable events. It is solely by the working of the Lord God, ministering to me that I, am able to have life victories. The power of the Holy Spirit by, which we are sealed with, seals us into the body of Christ.

I can testify, the Lord God, gives all necessary power by Christ, to emerge by the power in Christ's righteousness. In essence being sealed with the Holy Spirit, we are sealed with the Godhead, whose work is empowered, by the works of Christ Jesus.

As the Holy Spirit guides us into all truth, and fully testifies of the Lord Christ Jesus (the will of the Father). We are ministered to by God the Holy Spirit, to minister for God the Father, and Holy Spirit:

The privilege, I found in acquainting myself, with the Lord God, was in recognizing above all things. The Lord God, through the enabling, works of Christ is so much more than enough.

The Lord God is so much more than enough in loving, teaching, and leading my life. The Lord God, in ministering to me in love, uses the same provisions, the Lord Christ Jesus encourages us to use.

The heavenly Father, because of his love is using the full creative power of his Son, to defeat sin, in the lives of mankind. I can say without a doubt, the Lord God, who is, love, is so much more than enough.

Has provided for us through Christ Jesus, so much more than enough, to meet mankind's total need. In the promised work of the Lord Christ Jesus. Christ fulfilling his Father's assignment, is fully meeting mankind's total need.

The Lord Christ gives to his servants the same powerful provisions, which accompanied him. By which his servants are empowered, to minister for him.

Christ Jesus, led his disciples, to be aware. That they were called to minister. In what had been established. By those that served before them.

Which were the prophets. Who provided the gospel. The disciples, were. To minister with harmony. As led by the Holy Spirit, that inspired all the words, of the laborers:

"I sent you to reap that whereon ye bestowed no labour: **other men laboured, and ye are entered into their labours.** John 4:38"

"**The Lord gave the word: great was the company of those that published it. Psalms 68:11**"

"For the **prophecy came not** in old time **by the will of man:** but **holy men of God spake as they were moved by the Holy Ghost.** 2 Peter 1:21"

CHAPTER 8

SO MUCH MORE THAN ENOUGH

After all is said and done, it after all is about the Lord God. Who is indeed, so much more than enough. I see the Lord God, in love providing so much more than enough.

Just as the scripture promises, in retrospect I, see the Lord working. I, see all good things, and all perfect things come from acknowledging the Lord God:

> "The Lord is **my shepherd**; I shall not want. **He maketh me to lie down** in green pastures: **he leadeth me** beside the still waters. **He restoreth my soul: he leadeth me in the paths of righteousness for his name's sake.**
>
> Yea, though I walk through the valley of the shadow of death, I will **fear no evil**: for **thou art with me; thy rod and thy staff they comfort me.** Thou preparest a table before me in the presence of mine enemies: thou anointest my head with oil; **my cup runneth over.** Surely **goodness and**

> **mercy shall follow me** all the days of my life: **and I will dwell in the house of the Lord for ever.** Psalm 23:1-6"

I have found the Lord God is so much more than enough in being thorough in providing for mankind's needs. In all issues of life. Though walking in and through the dark. I see the Lord God's, love based, involvement, and intervention.

The Lord God, first of all, gives instruction, for actions that adds blessings to one's life. And the Lord gives instructions, by which to identify, and avoid things, and conditions that restrict the Lord's blessings.

I, see all good things, and all perfect things are by the Lord God. It is by and for the Lord all growth in my life is perpetuated by, and established through God's love.

I go to the Lord God, seeking to know him, but at the same time knowing, the Lord has control of what I can know. What the Lord God, makes known, is from love. And, I, see what the Lord God makes known is for us, to learn of his love.

I am confident, by attending upon what the Lord God says concerning himself, I am able to know him. I find God is revealed in his word, and in the tangible things revealed from creation.

Searching the word of God, is the Lord's way that mankind, can experience more of his greatness. Experiencing the Lord, in his word, leads me to know for certain the Lord's desire for me has not changed. I see the Lord God has expressed from the beginning that the Lord wants me to be like him.

It is clear, the Lord, planned for me, to live in humility. The Lord God's truth in his word fully expresses his humility. The Lord has taught me he wants me to seek his revealed truth, to obtain his righteous way:

> "The secret things belong unto the Lord our God: but those things which are revealed belong unto us and to our children for ever, **that we may do all the words of this law**. Deuteronomy 29:29"

The one thing, I, can say confidently, the Lord wants me to know him. I know without a doubt, the Lord God, desires for me to love him, and to know his love, and his works.

The Lord God leads mankind to know, love, and praise him. Love for the Lord by speaking of his works, and his daily wonders. I have grown to daily experience, doing as the Lord delights, is the delight of my soul:

> "I will extol thee, my God, O king; and I will bless thy name for ever and ever. Psalm 145:1"

I find it truly is a delight to bless the LORD God, which blesses me. I am blessed by the light of God's love. Ever before me even in and through the dark.

> "Every day will I bless thee; and I will praise thy name for ever and ever. Psalms 145:2"

As I bless the LORD, I am bathed in the rejoicing of why I want to bless the LORD, with praises:

> "Bless the Lord, O my soul: and all that is within me, bless his holy name. Bless the Lord, O my soul, and forget not all his benefits: Who forgiveth all thine iniquities; who healeth all thy diseases; Who redeemeth thy life from destruction; who crowneth thee with lovingkindness and tender mercies; Who satisfieth thy mouth with good things; so that thy youth is renewed like the eagle's. Psalms 103:1-5"

> "Great is the Lord, and greatly to be praised; and his greatness is unsearchable. One generation shall praise thy works to another, and shall declare thy mighty acts. Psalms 145:3-4"

I am so thankful for the opportunity to speak of the Lord, with praise of the Lord. The Lord God is the one I, seek to please. And before the Lord, I, rejoice for the opportunity to share him, to my children, family members, and friends.

> "I will speak of the glorious honour of thy majesty, and of thy wondrous works. Psalms 145:5"

I cannot believe how mankind, today being in varied dangers, in these perilous times, is not able to identify the Lord God's mercy. There are testimonies spoken, and visible, of the Lord God's merciful, deliverance.

Members of mankind from every nation have given public testimonies, through various media of their unexpected deliverance. Many I have heard sharing, 'I, thought I, was going to die'. Some media reports, show merciful rescues being made.

We have been able to hear thanksgiving, with praises to God being given by some person. Many persons praising the Lord. Are those who had been in the very face of death:

> "And men shall speak of the might of thy terrible acts: and
> I will declare thy greatness. Psalms 145:6"

I find delight in being led to create from the heart, songs from experiences I, personally have had by recognizing, how the Lord, has been, present, and active is in my life. Which leads me through the dark, by his provisions.

By remembering in retrospect, the Lord's hand of mercy, which is the way the Lord God, has made himself known to me. I created the following words, which I have shared with family and friends:

> "All the wrong that has happened in my life the Lord, is using for my good, yes x3. Just like he said he would, yes x3. All the wrong that has happened in my life the Lord, is using for my good.
>
> I can testify, the Lord, and his word is truth, by his word I abide, and in his promises, I thrive, because; Just like he said he would, yes x3 Yes, all the wrong that has happened in my life, the Lord, is using for my good. Just like he said he would (many times to fade out)"

As the following scripture verse concludes. It is the memory of the Lord's presence in my life that restores me. It is the memory of the Lord God's mercies in my life by the Holy Spirit's presence that keeps me growing in knowledge of the Lord:

> "They shall abundantly utter the memory of thy great goodness, and shall sing of thy righteousness. Psalms 145:7"

> "I will meditate in thy precepts, and have respect unto thy ways. I will delight myself in thy statutes: I will not forget thy word. Psalms 119:15-16"

What The Lord Has Done Testifies:

Truly I find, that which, the Lord God has done from the beginning, testifies of the Lord God. There is a steady flow of wonders shared, which cause there to be a rejoicing, in the work of God.

Even at a time of disasters, the Lord God's mercy is recognized. In the midst of loss, and sorrow, the Lord's presence has been confirmed. The Lord God steps in, and fulfilling his promises, he gives lasting hope:

> "The Lord is gracious, and full of compassion; slow to anger, and of great mercy. Psalms 145:8"

I have fully learned to rely upon the Lord, to fulfill his promises. When I go to him with my burdens, and labors, I, already know in his time the Lord fulfills all his promises. By responding to the Lord God's biding, increases my confidence in him:

> "Come unto me, all ye that labour and are heavy laden, and I will give you rest. Take my yoke upon you, and learn of me; for I am meek and lowly in heart: and ye shall find rest unto your souls. Matthew 11:28 -29"

"I would seek unto God, and unto God would I commit my cause: Which doeth great things and unsearchable; marvellous things without number: Job 5:8-9"

"The Lord is good to all: and his tender mercies are over all his works. Psalm 145:9"

The LORD for our knowledge, and observation, places before us reports of mankind being rescued by mankind. And on display also, is the care, which even animals do show for other animals.

"**All thy works shall praise thee**, O Lord; and thy saints shall bless thee. Psalms 145:10"

Chapter 9

Called and Set Apart

Saints, in scripture are recognized as all the persons, set apart to serve Christ Jesus. All persons that are sealed by the Holy Spirit.

The Lord God in his word, identifies the required way. And the people that follow the life example. And teachings of the Lord Christ.

> "They **shall speak of the glory of thy kingdom, and talk of thy power**; Psalms 145:11"

It is one of the Lord God's blessings, and constant encouragement, that mankind has at the time when they congregate together, that they share the love, faithfulness, and power of the Lord.

> "**To make known** to the sons of men his **mighty acts, and the glorious majesty of his kingdom**. Thy kingdom is an everlasting kingdom, and thy dominion endureth throughout all generations. Psalms 145:12 -13"

I receive so much joy, and encouragement, especially when I remember, the Lord's promise that the new earth's occupants shall be righteous.

> "But **the meek shall inherit the earth**; and shall delight themselves in the abundance of peace. Psalms 37:11"

All Soul's Needs Fulfilled By The Lord:

Knowing by confirmation, the great need of mankind is, and has been met by the Lord, God, establishes, and maintains my trust. It is to me, a deep trust, and heart comforting realization that I, can know God's will for me shall be fullfilled.

It keeps me encouraged that knowledge of the Lord God's love, and care for mankind. Is clearly spoken in the Lord's written, and living word.

I've learned the Lord continues, to fulfill, the way to prosper, and be in good health. When I recognized instruction in God's word to hear the Son for achieving God's will, I started searching.

I search the actions of Christ Jesus diligently, and listen to Christ's words attentively. By searching God's word, I, see Christ. For being my present help. I have learned the Lord Jesus, truly is the one who. Fulfills me, to walk God's talk.

> "Come unto me, all ye that labour and are heavy laden, and I will give you rest. Take my yoke upon you, and learn of me; for I am meek and lowly in heart: and ye shall find rest unto your souls. For my yoke is easy, and my burden is light. Matthew 11:28-30"

"The eyes of all wait upon thee; and thou givest them their meat in due season. Thou openest thine hand, and satisfiest the desire of every living thing. Psalms145:15-16"

"The Lord upholdeth all that fall, and raiseth up all those that be bowed down. Psalms 145:14"

Waiting On The Lord A Regular Need:

I, have learned, to fully rely upon the Lord to provide, all things, I, need to practice waiting. I, know it is beneficial to wait upon the Lord because he has promised.

I have learned I will be satisfied, from the result of waiting on the Lord. I, am still working on being still, after I have committed to waiting for the Lord, to fulfill my desires.

Waiting on the Lord's time, becomes easier, as I, remember how the Lord fulfills all his promises. And the Lord's promises being fulfilled, is in his time.

Knowing the Lord God's help, and comfort is in his word, I, know he says to wait. I, know I must remain committed to waiting patiently on the Lord, because his blessings are in the waiting. The most important reason for having the word of God, is to patiently live by what God's word says.

The word of God is the only way, to get to know the Lord God. To wait on the truth of what the Lord God, requires. Is to me the very act of patiently waiting on the Lord, before taking any action:

"Lead me in thy truth, and teach me: for thou art the God of my salvation; **on thee do I wait all the day.** Psalms 25:5"

"Let integrity and uprightness **preserve me; for I wait on thee.** Psalms 25:21"

"Wait on the Lord: be of good courage, and **he shall strengthen thine heart: wait, I say, on the Lord.** Psalms 27:14"

"But **they that wait upon the Lord shall renew their strength**; they shall mount up with wings as eagles; they shall run, and not be weary; and they shall walk, and not faint. Isaiah 40:3"

"And **therefore will the Lord wait, that he may be gracious unto you**, and therefore will he be exalted, that he may have mercy upon you: for the Lord is a God of judgment: **blessed are all they that wait for him.** Isaiah 30:18"

Forever Blessed By Christ:

My greatest comfort, which I have from the Lord God, involves claiming promises. I, have fully learned, it is Christ's integrity to fulfill his promises. The Lord Christ's promise to abide with me to give me help, rejoices my whole soul.

I, am involved in offering constant praise. My favorite way to praise the Lord, is by holding him up to others. And especially, by boasting of the Lord God's faithfulness, in fulfilling his promises.

The truth of living an abundant life, as I, have experienced, comes only, by abiding aware of the Lord Christ's promises. I know any peace, I am able to realize, comes by trusting in the Lord God's promises.

The present, and constant help I, am receiving from the Lord, is to me a constant rejoicing. I, find comfort in all the Lord's promises. The Lord's promises reveal to me, the Lord God, is, and is faithful in what he does, by confirmation.

During my time of putting forth effort, to know what my specific service to the Lord God would be. In my spirit, I saw the Lord's God's will more clearly, by his promises as I sought to know him:

> "Now I say that **Jesus Christ** was a minister of the circumcision for **the truth of God, to confirm the promises made unto the fathers:** Romans 15:8"

> "For **all the promises of God in him are yea, and in him Amen,** unto the glory of God by us. 2 Corinthians 1:20"

Desire To Serve God An Addiction:

From my desire to see, and serve the Lord God, more clearly. I have from effort, obtained a better vision, of the Lord Christ's leadership.

By me, desiring to grow in my knowledge of the Lord God, I, became addicted to scripture. Becoming addicted to the word of God, caused me to pursue, every subject, and situation of life with diligence using, the Holy scriptures. And the events in the lives of others.

In all my approaches it moved me to want to see from scripture, the Lord Christ's view. Knowing, that which Christ, had to say, and seeing, that which Christ lived, has priority for my life.

My gained knowledge of the Lord God, has prompted me, to keep, seeking, to know God. Searching scripture is a daily life practice for me. With the desire to make daily progress in knowing the Lord.

Christ's Life Answers The Questions:

The blessing I, discovered, in seeking what the Lord God, desired for me. I, found is clearly stated in the scriptures.

By searching the scripture, I, realized, the Lord God desires for me to know his Son. I, have been led by God's word to understand. The purpose, and will of God, was presented in the life of Christ Jesus.

The Lord Christ Jesus by his life example tells me, what the Heavenly Father, desired of me by saying, 'follow me'. The Lord Christ's life clarifies for me, the way that is God's saving health:

> "That **thy way may** be known upon earth, thy **saving health** among all nations. Psalms 67:2"

> "Jesus saith unto him, **I am the way**, the truth, and the life: no man cometh unto the Father, but by me. John 14:6"

Christ's Life Clarifies:

I, am led by all that was prophesied concerning Christ's purpose, and his work. Christ's life identifies to me how the Lord meets my need.

To serve the Lord God. I, have been led to see the Lord takes full control in equipping me. The Lord equips me with all that he requires of me. The Lord has well equipped me by telling me to follow him:

> "And he saith unto them, **Follow me, and I will make you** fishers of men. Matthew 4:19"

> "He **restoreth my soul**: he **leadeth me in the paths of righteousness** for his name's sake. Psalms 23:3"

I can now say with assurance, that which the Lord Christ, desires for me, is what I, desire for myself. I, can stand steadfast in Christ Jesus, because of the Lord's faithfulness. I find the Lord faithful in fulfilling his promises.

I, see truth was fully revealed in the gift of Christ Jesus. Truth was revealed to me, by the life of Christ. The Lord God's truth is found clearly affirmed, in God's word. And affirmed in the words, and life of Christ Jesus.

The witnessing of the disciples was of the life, and words of Christ Jesus. Keeping my growth in knowing and following Christ is my assurance, and safety.

The work of the disciples, is that which was given to other believing members of mankind. All those who accept Christ, are equipped, to live revealing Christ. To share the truth I, find I, must magnify the life, and work of Christ Jesus.

Building Life Eternal:

It is by the revelations throughout the scriptures, Old, and New testament, that I, am led to abide in following Christ. It is by seeking all doctrine surrounding Christ's life, that I, find is building true life for me.

Truth to me, is in the reality of Christ, being sent from the Father, as promised. The undeniable truth is proclaimed, by the Lord God's love-based purpose.

In the saving face of Christ Jesus, as it was foretold, Christ Jesus was sent. It was proven, Christ lived the way that promotes salvation. And Christ tells us to follow him.

The undeniable salvation gift for mankind in Christ. Centers on the soul of mankind having needs. Mankind has their soul needs met in totality (body, heart, mind, and spirit). Needs are fully met, by abiding in Christ.

Coming Of Christ Fulfills:

Christ the Lord, was sent, as prophesied, and for all nations. As by the comforting, prophesy of God sending salvation. In Christ God's purpose is being fulfilled to cover mankind's need.

By the Father sending his Son, the Lord Christ Jesus, we have the way, the truth, and the life. It is for mankind's eternal, profit that, the Lord God, tells mankind to hear his Son.

The promises, which the Lord God has given in his word, I, find are the things righteousness seeking mankind desires. Christ daily lived, preached, and Christ as the leader of righteousness, taught the way. The fruit, I, seek to produce in my life, is all presented in the promises of the Lord God:

> "But **seek ye first the kingdom of God, and his righteousness**; and all these things shall be added unto you. Matthew 6:33"

> "And Jesus said unto them, Come ye after me, and **I will make you to become fishers of men.** Mark 1:17"

> "But as many as received him, to them **gave he power to become the sons of God,** even to them that believe on his name: John 1:12"

Godhead Works Together:

The Father promised the Holy Spirit, by which we are taught all things. The word of God being inspired, by the Holy Spirit, leads us by testifying of, and pointing to truth, which is the Lord Christ Jesus.

As the scriptures has revealed. The three members of the Godhead work together on our behalf. I see the Father loving us, and sending Christ Jesus.

The Father from the beginning testifies of his Son. By the Father proclaiming his Son in his kinsman Redeemer, role for mankind, we were prepared for Christ to enter our individual lives.

I see the Lord Christ Jesus, in love for his Father. And in love for mankind, humbly submitting himself. All the way through to the cross. I, see Christ by submission, to his Father, fulfilling the law, and the prophets.

In Christ's works of salvation, he glorified his Father, and his Father's love. Christ clarified the fulfillment of his role, as he gave the good news:

> "The Spirit of the Lord is upon me, because **he hath anointed me to preach the gospel to the poor; he hath sent me to heal the brokenhearted, to preach deliverance** to the captives, and recovering of sight to the blind, **to set at liberty them that are bruised,** Luke 4:18"

> "For **God so loved the world, that he gave his only begotten Son,** that **whosoever believeth in him should not perish, but have everlasting life**. For God sent not his Son into the world to condemn the world; but **that the world through him might be saved.** John 3:16-17"

The Holy Spirit, I, see is the one person that if spoken against, could cause a person to perish. The Holy Spirit is the member of the Godhead that inspired, and uses the word. To teach and exalt Christ Jesus.

The members of the body of Christ, being prepared for service by the Holy Spirit, is what identifies Christ's believers. The gift of the Holy Spirit to Christ's church body, is part of the Lord God's plan as promised:

> "And we know that **the Son of God is come,** and hath given us an understanding, **that we may know him that is true,** and **we are in him that is true,** even in his Son Jesus Christ. **This is the true God, and eternal life.** 1 John 5:20"

As I read of the Lord God's works, I am able also in my mind to apply experiences I've had, which confirm, the Holy Spirit's presence in my life. I have been able by the Holy Spirit's guidance to connect promises being confirmed.

Through many experiences, in my life being confirmed, I, am forever comforted. Confirmations from the Lord, contributes to my joy in the Lord.

I, see myself spending my time devoted to identifying the fulfillment of the Lord's promises. I see myself continually growing in knowledge of the Lord, with the hope of blessing other's lives as I minister.

Seeing the Lord God, is the same (Father, Son, and Holy Spirit), is that, which secures my comfort, and growing confidence in the Lord God. The constant assurance, I have of the Lord God being so much more than enough.

Is from the realization of the constant evidence, and confirmation experiences, of God's presence. I, have full assurance of the Lord God's confirmed faithfulness.

From the experiences I, have in my life I, am led to trust the Lord God. I, am comforted as well, as I, observe confirmations being made, in regards to the lives of others.

I, receive confirmation, by the word, that the Godhead, is faithfully involved in my life. And from observation, it is evident to me that, the Lord God is involved in the lives of all members of mankind.

As I, am drawn to see the Lord God, I see him available, with a present invitation. All persons, of all nations have the same gracious invitation, to know the love of the Lord God, revealed in the working of the Godhead.

Knowledge of the Lord God, is best obtained by knowing, and accepting the life of the Son, Christ Jesus.

I see in the life of the Lord Christ Jesus, a constant reaching out. for all mankind to come to him. And by the inspired word of truth, to discover, and find peace, in knowing Christ as the Kinsman, Redeemer.

The comfort I, receive, is of Christ's desire, for his church body, to have a part in adding members to his church body. By abiding in, and having fellowship with Christ, God's Son, I am better able to identify, the needs of others.

By meditating day, and night, on what the Lord, has revealed in his word, I, am removed from earth's drama. By keeping my mind steadfast in abiding in Christ. I, remove from my mind. Whatsoever is not of the Lord God:

"This book of **the law shall not depart out of thy mouth**; but thou shalt **meditate therein day and night**, that thou mayest **observe to do according to all that is written** therein: for then thou shalt **make thy way prosperous**, and then thou shalt **have good success.** Joshua 1:8"

"I will **meditate also of all thy work, and talk of thy doings.** Psalms 77:12"

CHAPTER 10

Sudden Sorrow

At the very beginning of 2019, we received messages of two family member's passing. Though we felt sorrow, for our, 69, year-old nephew's passing, it appeared to be more of a natural mourning period.

We were comforted by knowing our nephew Jimmy Johnson, had trusted in the Lord. And even as the hand of death was gripping him. Jimmy knew in Christ Jesus, he had nothing to lose.

Jimmy's final words for us were, "See you on the other side". "Remember me". By our nephew, being known for a few years, to have a probable terminal condition (colon cancer). Jimmy's early life passing was easier accepted, all though it was sorrowful, it was not shocking.

A Deeper Sorrow:

A day following the report of our nephew's, passing, we, received a heart rending, report, concerning our much, loved niece Traci. Our niece's, and our children's cousin's passing, due to being without answers was, unexpected, and instantly heartbreaking.

We, for little over a year, had obtained a renewed contact with Traci, and had formed a close relationship with our niece Traci. And our youngest daughter Kim, especially talked with her cousin Traci, often by phone, hearing her voice, for over a year.

The sharing of current situations, and having opportunities to Learn about one another, and sharing joys of the past, was a treasure. There had been the free, flowing contact by phone, and texting, which Kim had.

Our niece Traci, and myself, frequently had spiritual, and life strengthening, communication, using texted messages, and emails. Traci, and I, formed a very close, and heart touching relationship.

Due to the growing trust in the Lord from questions asked, and ideas shared I, felt Traci, increasing in the joy of the lord. Traci, who had a special bond with her mom, that had passed years ago. Traci, was refreshed after asking me how did I, see her mom.

I, was thankful that some hardships, and disadvantages she thought her mom had to bear, I, was able to give a different picture, then what Traci thought about the constant church work her mom had been involved with.

I, had good memories to share, based on what her mom, my friend Mercedes, often shared with me. We by our spiritual sharing, were building a sound, and trusting relationship.

And then there was that day when, by email we received a sudden report of our 55, year old, niece Traci, being in a coma.

The report grew worse with the report of a bleeding brain. And then the very worse, and heart, rending report. Of our niece Traci, being 'on a ventilator, and a DNR, order' by request of her father.

The report on our Traci's condition. Was hard to take, I could say the report was. Very devastating, and disheartening. The hardest part of the situation. Was that of not having our question, 'what happened?', answered.

'What happened?' was not answered to any degree of satisfaction, which was discomforting for us. 'What happened' was the question asked by many family members, and friends.

It was because of not receiving, information concerning, our niece's sudden illness? or injury? We, along with other family members, and friends, felt bewildered, sorrowful, hurt, and even angry.

Some members, of the family even started immediately expressing some very strong feelings of resentment. "Why is God taking the young ones, and leaving the old ones". Was even the communication expressed, by younger family members to our sister-in-law, Grace, at the time in her 90's.

The only information available prompted a bitter response, 'she was just thrown away', was one repeated, broken heart expressions. The questions kept coming, 'what happened?'

There wasn't any clear answers to give, from no clear answer to the questions being asked. Wanting to know, what happened, is a natural heart, yearning response, from those left behind by death.

Even people hearing about the situation, wanted to know, 'what happened?'. Many prayer warriors were involved. Who, though having a part in praying, could not, with passing of time be informed of, 'what happened'.

And though we, prayed, 'God's will be done,' we, were looking for a miracle. And there were also many prayers by friends for our niece's recovery, and healing.

One of the important things involving any loss, is the need to have a closure. Not having definite answers, to a simple question. Prevented a healthy closure from occurring.

The Lord Keep's His Comforting Promise:

From seeking the Lord, I, was comforted by the Lord's promise to help us through the difficult things of life. I, was also helped by the word of God.

I, found God's word describes all, the things to expect can happen in our world, and why. The word of God as promised, answered the need of our heart that was overcome by sorrow:

> "These **things I have spoken unto you, that in me ye might have peace.** In the world ye shall have tribulation: but be of good cheer; I have overcome the world. John 16:33"

"Peace I leave with you, **my peace I give unto you: not as the world giveth, give I unto you**. Let not your heart be troubled, neither let it be afraid. John 14:27"

"**Casting all your care upon him**; for he careth for you. 1 Peter 5:7"

The Answer From Jesus Prior To His Death:

Christ Jesus our perfect shepherd gave the disciples, a full report of the things that would happen, to him. The disciples were prepared by Christ giving them full information involving his suffering, death, and resurrection.

And Christ also gave a clear report prior to the cruel treatment, and his death. Christ also gave report of his resurrection from death, which should have eased the disciples sorrow, yet they deeply sorrowed.

Because the disciples held on to the outward appearance, they leaned on their own understanding. We were responding to our niece's death, due to the outward appearance.

Good encouragement came to me from God's word. I sought the Lord with purpose, and he answered my concern:

"Trust in the Lord with all thine heart; and lean not unto thine own understanding. Proverbs 3:5"

The Lord's Faithfulness:

I, had no doubt that comfort could, and would come from the Lord. As at other times, early in the morning, in my spirit, I, received words from scripture, 'for sorrow'.

Remembering the brief clarification, in scripture regarding the reaction of the disciples closest to Christ. I started receiving an understanding, of reactions of relatives closer in relationship to our niece. Why they did not provide a full report of what had happened:

> "And being in an agony he prayed more earnestly: and his sweat was as it were great drops of blood falling down to the ground. And when he rose up from prayer, and was come to his disciples, **he found them sleeping for sorrow**, And said unto them, Why sleep ye? rise and pray, lest ye enter into temptation. Luke 22:44-46"

It was when Jesus expressed disappointment to his disciples of them not able to watch with him. The Lord asked the disciples a question, in his sorrow.

And the disciples he asked to watch, did not give an answer, because they were in sorrow. The Lord being faithful, gave me answers, with additional teaching, due to our need.

One of the reasons why I have learned to fully trust Christ. I, have learned when I seek answers from the Lord, I receive comfort, and valuable teaching.

The guidance that, I, have received from the word of the Lord, comforts me. And the Lord has taught me many important things, from this sorrowful event, involving our niece, Traci:

> "Sorrow is better than laughter: for by the sadness of the countenance the heart is made better. Ecclesiastes 7:3"

A Profitable Practice:

Since 1996, I, have used the prompting from God's word, to see what God has to say, concerning anything. And as I, have benefitted from experiences, I, go to the Lord.

I, have approached the word, concerning everything that, happens in our world. I, also remember the Lord's invitation, to give him all my burdens, and all my labors.

With the Lord's promise to give his peace, and rest. My, heart being comforted by the Lord, started to be realized. In my spirit, I, received answer, to the lack of answers involving, the death of our niece.

And I, started moving from feeling burdened by needing to know, to the satisfaction of the Lord God, showing me, many answers to my concern.

Upon issues surrounding Christ's preparation for death, and the reactions of the disciples. 'for sorrow', was the response that came to my spirit.

And the situation we were troubled by, immediately turned into a teaching message from the Lord. I, was encouraged by just the words, 'of sorrow' of how Christ, and the Father sees situations.

My practice of trusting the Lord, and going to God's word, as instructed paid-off. I was comforted by my expectation, from trusting the Lord God, to do just as he promised.

Difference Between God And Mankind:

Something so comforting to me, which, I, shared with family, and many prayer warriors. The Lord see's the heart of every matter.

The Lord sees the heart of every person. And the Lord God knows the reason, and intensions of each person. And each person's response is known by the Lord. Even though the persons themselves may not be fully cognizant of their own response:

> "But Jesus did not commit himself unto them, because **he knew all men,** And needed not that any should testify of man: for **he knew what was in man.** John 2:24-25"

Mankind in the flesh, looks at situations, and thinks about events, according to the outward appearance. Mankind in essence sees with the flesh, which often leads his spirit to be led by the flesh. We are blessed by having the Lord God, to guide us in our thoughts, and actions.

The Lord is ready to intervene to redirect us according to our need. The Lord knowing the spirit of the flesh we occupy, encourages us to go to him, with our all:

"For **he knoweth our frame**; he remembereth that we are dust. Psalm 103:14"

"**Come, ye children,** hearken unto me: **I will teach you the fear of the Lord.** Psalms 34:11"

"**Come unto me**, all ye that labour and are heavy laden, and **I will give you rest.** Matthew 11:28"

CHAPTER 11

Ready and Set to Go

I am encouraged by the fact that, the Lord prepares. I feel I have gained the feeling of being, set free. To use my total self freely, in serving the Lord God. I, know I have learned, and gained so much more than enough. From ongoing help from the Lord.

The Lord has prepared me to reach out freely in serving the Lord God. I especially enjoy the following scripture verses. The following scriptures, gives me a revelation, of my desired relationship, with the Lord God.

clear to me. The Lord God always goes before us. The Lord I, can see has always been before me, and he guides me into desiring to serve in the way he has appointed:

> "And the king's servants said unto the king, Behold, **thy servants are ready to do whatsoever my lord the king shall appoint** 2 Samuel 15:15."

"Behold, I send an Angel before thee, **to keep thee in the way, and to bring thee into the place which I have prepared.** Exodus 23:20"

Ready To Face Diversity:

One of the things, which I feel has given me a greater desire, to even interact with people of diverse beliefs, is my belief in God's word. I believe what the Lord Christ has taught, and lived:

> "**No weapon that is formed against thee shall prosper;** and every tongue that shall rise against thee in judgment thou shalt condemn. **This is the heritage of the servants of the Lord, and their righteousness is of me**, saith the Lord. Isaiah 54:17"

> "Know ye not, that **to whom ye yield yourselves servants to obey, his servants ye are to whom ye obey;** whether of sin unto death, or of obedience unto righteousness? Romans 6:16"

> "Being then made free from sin, **ye became the servants of righteousness.** Romans 6:18"

> "But now being made free from sin, and become servants to God, **ye have your fruit unto holiness, and the end everlasting life.** Romans 6:22"

And I believe, I, can do all things through Christ Jesus' life strengthening provisions. My confidence sours, as I, recall, and know without a doubt, that I, have the power of present help:

"But **as many as received him, to them gave he power to become the sons of God**, even to them that believe on his name: John 1:12"

"In whom **ye also trusted, after that ye heard the word of truth,** the gospel of your salvation: in whom also after that ye believed, ye were sealed with that holy Spirit of promise, Ephesians 1:13"

The Holy Spirit indwells me and goes everywhere with me teaching me. I, feel the promises being proven true, with confirmations, from the word of God.

"For we are his workmanship, **created in Christ Jesus unto good works**, which God hath before ordained that we should walk in them. Ephesians 2:10"

Chapter 12

A Blessed Conversation

I can still hear the question from our youngest daughter, Kim, "Mother, what are you doing with your sign language?" From that day I, was prompted by Kim. Things started happening involving my dedicated to use sign language in ministry.

Before moving to Arizona, I, had a job in California. A Supervisor on a deaf unit. which required for me to be somewhat fluent in Sign language.

In CA. I had passed a state examination, which allowed me, to be recognized as an interpreter, for the Deaf. I, enjoyed using sign language, with total-Communication, in every way I could.

I, especially enjoyed using, 'Signing Exact English', which allowed me to sign every concept of a message. Signing every known word when presenting a song really enhanced the worship in song for myself, and many others.

The signed concept of, the song's gospel message, by movement and by song. Added to the purpose for worshipping the Lord. It was an expressed appreciation by many who were presented with that form of language.

The Word Of God Enriches:

One of my greatest blessings for growing, in knowledge of the Lord, came when I, stated signing scripture. My purpose at first in signing scripture verses, was to build my knowledge in the language of signing.

I, had purchased, all the available, sign language books, to use for reference. My first my use of sign language outside of a job, was in the church. To the delight of many my first use of sign language in church, was with the presentation of a song.

My purpose of using songs, was to answer my daughter Kim's question, "Mother, what are you doing with your sign language?"

The church we were attending, had occasional visits by people that were deaf. At the time of our early attendance of the church, there was a person signing for the deaf visitors.

The previous interpreter moved away. And I was given the opportunity, to be the interpreter for the deaf worshippers. Becoming an interpreter for the deaf, led me, to create, a way to include all members.

I, developed, an enjoyable, and purposeful way to acquaint all members, and visitors of the church. To the beauty of sign language, as a spiritually gifted language from God.

I, received from many of the church members a positive response, to my efforts. Recognizing the church member's need, fired me up for service, which included using God's word, along with the songs.

Seeking to bless the people, and serve the Lord. I, sought ways to bless all persons in the congregation. It was like finding, and providing treasure. I, sought every opportunity to use God's word with sign language.

Being given the title, 'Deaf Ministries', prepared me to bless, and also be a recipient of blessings. Using a less than 5 min period, at the break of lesson study, was proven to have blessed many with direct focus on God.

During the period, when nothing was being provided. Allowed, a short but joyful, time for direct worship towards the Lord. A Love to God focused worship period using sign language. Also provided an increased in using, and learning God's word.

It was a blessing to fill the usual empty time, first by me, signing a song, using total communication (signing and verbalizing). The song was followed by signing the word of God, which the congregation repeated with me.

Deaf Ministry Advanced To Special Music:

One of my most soul refreshing use of sign language, involved performing worship songs, in a group. The ministry required interested church members to meet, and learn signs.

Signs were learned and performed to go along with recorded songs, which all were directed towards the Lord. There were two performances provided each month during church service.

I, am today thankful for the willing, and interested persons, besides myself. My husband Bob, with good perceptual movement skills also enjoyed taking part is signing to the songs.

Another married couple, Delroy, and Rose Clarke, were an active pair, devoted to worship, and also enjoyed the signing experience. Other interested members, of 'Deaf' ministries included, Angela Harper, Rosemary Kennedy, Margaret Roomes, and Victoria Miles.

Angela, who had a background in signing, and was helpful in keeping enthusiasm going. Rosemary Kennedy, brought a refreshing appreciation, of having a part in that which to her was a new movement expression to which she had to adapt.

By Rosemary's reactions, one could appreciate the total affect, the movement expression, could have upon a person. Signing was a challenge, in which I know from observation, Rosemary found delight.

Margret Roomes, was always willing to have a part in any new challenge, and no matter what. Margaret, was a willing participant.

Victoria Miles, graciously welcomed the new opportunity to learn. Vicky's participation in the new language for worship, was always perfect with her performance. I, remember Vicky sharing when she was driving, and had occasion to pause, she would practice the signs.

Importance Of Word Additions:

I also learned to see sign language as a great asset to be guarded. I, learned to teach members, and other people, to avoid the use of street signs.

It is a natural thing to be influenced by others, wanting to demonstrate their knowledge of some signs. Effort to avoid receiving the demonstration, of profanity. And other words to taint signing vocabulary, is important.

Like any language there are signs to avoid if the intention is to serve God, and others. I found it necessary to guard against the use of some words. Performing with movement by the uniqueness of sign language. Does impact the whole person.

Worshipping the Lord, with synchronized movements, by signing. Is a definite way to capture the heart. Sign language is a good, and beautiful art-form. For use in worshipping the Lord God. And proper use, strengthens the thinking for good.

Undesirable sharing of signs, would appear. Being approached by persons anxious to share signs. Was a learning, and teaching experience for me.

The experience of recognizing the power of words even signed taught me. From identifying the power of signed words. I, realized signs could also be used for not so good.

I, saw the movements of signing. Work as a seal on my total soul. It prepared me to communicate. The blessings of signing. That helps to promote. And maintain good thoughts. I would encourage people, "It engraves God's word on the soul".

Interest in sign language. Also opened the door for me to preach. It gave the opportunity. To identify the need for God's word. I, experienced the reality. Of why we, should always consider God's counsel. The Lord in wisdom leads us. To keep us away from the dark. Especially as we sign.

Seeking to acknowledge the Lord with signs. I, learned guided me in making wise choices. The Lord's counsels, has kept from dark. As I, sought the Lord's way.

All the songs that were used. Gave direct praise to the Lord. I, And I, am blessed just from the memory. Of the signed words, that were used for the ministry.

The music that was chosen. Was used to bless, the Lord. The congregation and ourselves. I, remember the first song. We, started off with was, "**Almighty I Surrender**" (voice, Damaris Carbaugh),

> "You are crowned in majesty, You are clothed in glory, You are pure and holy and God. Yet you gave your Son, to me, sacrificed on Calvary. This your greatest mystery that you could love me. Almighty, God, Creator, Redeemer, Liberator, Eternal Lord, and Savior, God. My Father, my Defender, my broken heart mender. Lord Jesus I, surrender all, you are God, you are God."

Another song that toughed the soul: '**Knowing You Jesus**,' (voice Matthew Ward), "All I once held dear, Built my life upon. All this world reveres And wants to own. All I once thought gain

I have counted loss Spent and worthless now Compared to this. Knowing You Jesus, knowing You, There is no greater thing. You're my all, You're the best, You're my joy, my righteousness. And I love You Lord."

The Start Of "Visual Testimony":

I, soon was led to create a signing ministry, 'Visual Testimony'. It allowed the public sharing of songs. To encourage the worship of the Lord God. The ministry also allowed, an opportunity for creating awareness. Of the needs of the deaf community. And aging the members of a community.

"Visual Testimony" was an outreach for songs of praise. And related scripture verses. 'Visual Testimony', had the main purpose. Of giving praise, and honor to the Lord God.

Visual Testimony, fell to the wayside. But it has proven, to be a preparatory step. Signing to praise the Lord. Goes with me where ever I worship. And has led the way for me. To grow in seeking, knowing, and serving the Lord.

CHAPTER 13

PREPARED FOR A FRIEND

Attending a mid-week daytime bible study, at a Missionary, Baptist Church. When asked what our gifts were. I shared, and the ministers of the church became very interested that, I had signing ability. 'Maybe you, can help us?'

I, was told of a lady that was attending the church who was deaf. And though no one was interpreting the message for her, she kept attending the church services.

I, met Irene, and was informed, it was the loud vibrating music (especially the drums) that had drawn Irene to attend that particular church. The loud music vibrations kept Irene going, to the Missionary Baptist church.

The church also had the practice of sharing bible verse. And all the bible scripture verses were shared on a screen. Irene, would note the location of the verses shared. To later look-up in her bible. Looking at Irene's notes. I, could see Irene's love of God's word. Irene had accumulated many scripture verses.

Meeting Irene A Joy:

The first time I, interpreted for Irene. Many of the church members wanted me to stand where all members could benefit. But it was not advisable for me. To respond to their request.

It was ideal if around a deaf person. To have the opportunity to learn signing. Yet being up close, and attentive to Irene. For question, and answer signing. Was what Irene, and I, both needed.

The very first time I, met with Irene. I, felt from her a strong desire to grow. In her knowledge of, and relationship with the Lord. I, recognized immediately, Irene would benefit from active participation.

I, encouraged Irene, to sign what was presented, in song or verse, along with me. Using total communication (signing and speaking). I, signed the message, and church announcements.

Irene gave me a compliment. That touched my heart. and blessed me a lot. Irene signed to me, "You are a kind person".

Irene's compliment, meant so much, to me. And as I, signed I, was grateful, to serve Irene.

I, was aware by Irene's body, and facial expressions. Irene, possessed a special sensitivity. To what was happening around her. A respectful heart bonding. Between us was also evident.

Caring Goes With Serving:

I, care about you, has to be the message. Care is communicated, in various ways. I, have found from my past people serving occupations. It becomes a natural response for me. To feel the needs, and concerns of anyone I, am assisting.

I, also have learned to totally depend upon the Lord. Whenever, any up-close assistance is afforded me. I, know it was just not being friendly, and saying nice words. That bonded Irene, and I together. It was the Lord's consideration an care for us both.

God's Spirit showed up, and was identified. In every encounter. To bring someone closer to him. The Lord works many ways.

Having the need to express gratitude. And welcoming the opportunity to be of help. It is all for the Lord. And it is from the Lord God:

> "The liberal soul shall be made fat: and **he that watereth shall be watered also himself**. Proverbs 11:25"

'I, will try to please you', was signed by Irene. which helped me Identify a need. I, felt the Lord wanted to meet Irene's need. By communicating the Lord. Was the only one to please. 'Irene you do what you do, to please God, not me'.

'God is the focus, and the Lord God is the one who provides the help we need'. Trust God, for all your needs, was a constant communication to Irene. Which was either written, or signed.

One thing Irene, let me know. Concerning the deaf community (she evidently felt unique). Gossip was a thing, Irene, felt went along with the deaf. And Irene, hated gossip.

Irene also let me know. There was a lot of control in the deaf community. She shared there was a lot. Of pressure in the deaf community. Where a group, would pressure one person.

Irene, felt so many of the deaf community needed to know the Lord. Irene wanted more deaf people to be Christian. And Irene desired to have. A closer relationship with the Lord.

Another Doctrine Based Rejection:

One of the things, the Lord, had prepared me for, was more rejection. I, had already learned, if I, was not wholeheartedly accepting a churches doctrine. I, would be targeted as an enemy.

The oddest experience we, encountered at the weekly bible study. Pastor Friend, had asked the question, 'how much time did members spend in the bible.

After I, shared that my study of the bible was daily. Pastor Friend's reaction indicated. That he was a bit angered. And did not accept my answer. Bob guaranteed the pastor I, was in the bible daily.

And the Pastor never changed his expression of disbelief, and resentment. 'if one would tell the truth'. Was a quick response by Pastor Friend.

I, noticed when the church leaders expected for us to join. As they were, informed we did not join any church. The church leaders, and some of the members. Were not pleased by that revelation either.

Questions Seen As Threats:

On one occasion a sermon was given with such remarks as, 'tell your neighbor, I, got your back'. 'Look at your neighbor, and just stare'.

When it was sermon time. A group of members were randomly selected to stand at the front of the church. They stood with their arms entwined with one another (in a resisting stance). There was a member attempting to break into group.

The resisting group, was encouraged. To keep a person from entering the group. The person selected was encouraged. To forcefully enter the struggling group. Or to break the group apart.

There was a lack of verbal specifics by the Pastor. Concerning the group drama. Upon our next attendance of bible study. I, asked the question, 'what did that illustration represent?

I, received no answer to my question concerning the drama. Therefore, I, shared with the Pastor, what I, had gotten out of the group's activity. From the what I, had viewed from Access TV.

I, shared a church add I, had watched on Access TV. The ad showed a boy with his dog enter a church. And after a few moments. The dog was being led out. By an apparent church leader.

The impact of the TV ad. Was seeing sandaled feet over draped by a robe. Coming up to the dog. And with comforting words stating, 'It's okay, they won't let me in either'.

Nothing was said by Pastor Friend. To whom. I, had made my observation. There were other times during bible study. When, I would make a comment that was bible based. Yet treated as false even though Christ. Shown to have been teaching.

I, again received indication. By facial, and body language expressions. My attempts to share bible basics. Was often met with a show of resentment. I, recognize again resentment, of God's word.

I, remember stating, 'I felt from being an avid student of the scriptures. That it was impossible for me to doubt God. Later, I learned by another clear drama. My comment, concerning not doubting God. Was without a doubt recented.

Anger Dressed In Chains:

My last day of interpreting for Irene. At that missionary Baptist church was dramatic. When it came time for the sermon. The minister of music (who wanted to be called Reverend), came out of the Pastor's study.

As the minister moved forward. It was clearly noticed. Over the minister's suit, he was wrapped in chains. And the chains were leading to a suitcase. The minister of music walking laboriously. Drug the suitcase to the pulpit.

Hostility Not Hidden:

My deaf, friend Irene, being sensitive. To body, and facial language. Irene kept her eyes on the minister of music. Irene, had an expression of concern on her face. Irene with eye shifting. Communicated to me she, was concerned.

From the obviously questionable appearance. Of the minister of music. The way he entered the sanctuary. Was without a doubt. An unusual presentation.

The ministers dress indicated. He was carrying a burden. At the sermon's start I, received indications. From him that he needed to unload on me. He ended his accusatory sermon, with 'bye, bye'.

Now I know the unusual presentation was prepared to communicate. A strong objection to me. Due to my bible use as reference. During a bible lesson study

The minister of music by associations. Apparently planned to create an uneasiness for me.

Irene by body, and facial language. Communicated She had great concern. The minister of music's very first words (which I, interpreted). Told me I, personally was the subject.

Irene, with facial expressions. Identified she sensed bad vibes. The minister started, 'first of all I, want you to know. It's okay for you to doubt, God'.

I, picked up right away. The prepared drama, was against me. The ministered used words of a song. I, had just recently up loaded to YouTube. The song which I, sang, and signed. Was, 'From The Rising Of The Sun'.

All the way through the very strongly hostile message. To the, final ending of, 'Bye, Bye'. And I, signed every accusatory word. All the way through as it was spoken. Interpreting by signs the accusatory hostility.

I, was by signing the whole to Irene. And Irene with her gift from being deaf. Was interpreting the visual display. Of accusatory hostility, directed towards me.

The dismayed, expressions were eased. From Irene's face and body language. As Irene noticed my relaxed calmness. As I signed every hostile accusatory word.

I, believe the actions of the minister of music. Were of value, which help identify to Irene. The reason why, I, had counseled her. That God was the only one. In our life we strive to please.

From my first encounter with Irene. The Lord opened me to Irene's most immediate need. Giving Irene the constant focus. On striving to please the Lord God alone. Added strength, to both of our lives.

Having a growing relationship with the Lord God. Was Irene's, expressed desire. Irene, also expressed. She wanted to minister for the Lord.

With Irene desiring to serve God. The Lord God led me to see. A way to meet Irene's need. Assisting Irene, helped my growth.

As the music minister gave his talk. It gave me insight to him. Lacking knowledge of the main scriptures. Christ named the all the Old Testament books. That were to be searched. I pray for, the Minister of music today.

The statement given by the minister of music. Was as stated. 'The old Testament, and the New Testament, are completely different books, they are 'no way alike'. Another reason why I, have need. For God's faithful word that instructs me. Through, and in the dark:

> "Jesus answered and said unto them, **Ye do err, not knowing the scriptures,** nor the power of God. Matthew 22:29"

I, reminded the minister of the words of Jesus. Involving the Old Testament, and himself. The minister of music, just reluctantly nodded. Quickly moving his head sideways. He made no self-justifying comment.

It was clear to me the reason. There was objection to the things. I, shared in sincerity. I, thrive by God's grace for any moment. He allows me to know the need. For all subjects taught to be supported. By God's truth illuminating word.

There is a definite way to clarify any subject. By faithfully searching God's word. And to treasure the word through, and in the dark. As the light to live by, for the support of truth.

Christ being my leader has taught me. As long as I, live in this world. I shall need his word. The Lord has led me to acknowledge all the prophets. Who by inspiration of the Holy Spirit. Provides the power to move. Through, and in the dark:

"And beginning at **Moses and all the prophets, he expounded unto them in all the scriptures the things concerning himself.** Luke 24:27"

"For **had ye believed Moses**, ye would have believed me: for **he wrote of me.** John 5:46"

"Abraham saith unto him, **They have Moses and the prophets; let them hear them.** Luke 16:29"

"And he said unto him, **If they hear not Moses and the prophets,** neither will they be persuaded, though one rose from the dead. Luke 16:31"

Better Things For Irene:

I, informed Irene of the Missionary Baptist church. Not wanting my presence there. Irene, immediately made her decision. She would no longer attend. Worship at that church. And Irene found other places. Where the deaf could worship.

Need For Worship:

Irene, was attending a midweek deaf taught bible study group. Taught by a deaf friend Roxane Fenicle, along with a few other deaf friends. The deaf minister, Roxane, was looking for a place. Where the group could meet.

I, thought of, a place could possibly share a space. I, asked Pastor Otis Brown Jr, and he was pleased, to share space. Not being used in his church.

On the Sunday the deaf group visited. I, was there to assist with needed interpretation. I, signed for the group, the message given by Pastor Otis Brown. I, signed everything that was presented.

I recall Roxane signing to me after. That I, had signed straight for over 2 hours. A concern Roxane had by being a deaf instructor (Deaf Missions). I, learned, and have made some change. Roxane also was suggesting. That I use 'easier' signs.

The deaf minister Roxane Fenicle, decided not to use the available space. Deaf parents, I, learned had hearing Children. And with plans for the children to attend. It called for a different setting.

A Worship Place For Irene':

Irene, was encouraged from Pastor Brown's message. Irene realized she could worship. And receive bible study at Siloam Freewill Church. If I, would interpret for her.

Irene, communicated to me her desire. And worship for Irene at Siloam Freewill Church. Began for Irene, the next week. I, could see Irene was pleased. And was encouraged, by Pastor Brown's sermon. And Irene was warmly accepted, by the church members.

Signing the songs again with me. I could see encouraged Irene more. Worship together blessed both Irene, and myself. Because we both had the same desire. To more fully know, and serve the Lord.

Irene brought with her, an expression of joy. Each time we met to worship the Lord. Irene, also benefitted by having. A fill-in sermon hand-out. Provided by Pastor Brown.

Irene enjoyed signing with me. And using advanced signs, same as I. As I, interpreted the words of songs. And any scripture verses that were posted. Irene followed, the worship service, intently.

Bob, and I, attended Pastor Brown's church. To allow Irene, to enjoy worship. And to encourage Irene, in active worship. Along with the congregation.

Bob and I, also enjoyed sharing meals. Restaurant outings also allowed the sharing. Of more regular, and daily signs.

A Difficult Period:

The previous information, that Irene had given me. Concerning the control in the deaf community. Came to fruition.

Disapproval by the deaf community over Irene's desire to use more advanced ASL was expressed to Irene. Following the deaf group's visit to Pastor Brown's church. Irene, was growingly disturbed.

Irene, communicated she was experiencing. Disapproval from the deaf community, over Irene's choice to have, my, advanced signs, interpreted, for worship.

The way I, was signing was what Irene, desired to keep progressing towards. Irene was increasing knowledge. By the use of more advanced signs.

It was felt by the deaf community, Irene, needed to stay with simple signs. And, to go for more advanced signs, would not be good for Irene. It, became a decision, that Irene, had to make.

The ultimatum to choose between advanced ASL. And the deaf community's approval. Irene had to decide on whether to continue her attendance, at Pastor Brown's. Or go to somewhere, else. Irene with prayer decided she wanted. The more advance ASL that I, provided:

> "In all thy ways **acknowledge him, and he shall direct** thy paths. Proverbs 3:6"

> "In my distress **I cried unto the Lord**, and he heard me. Psalms 120:1"

> "My help cometh from the Lord, which made heaven and earth. Psalms 121:2"

Opportunity To Minister:

From Irene, expressing her desire to serve God. A way was provided for Irene. By giving her a space, on my, YouTube channel. Irene, had a section entitled, "Irene Neal A Deaf Friend".

Irene in starting her ministry. Introduced herself as a deaf Christian. Irene let viewers know she loved the Lord, and those viewing. Love for the viewers. Was expressed in all of Irene's messages:

Irene's messages were short and to the point. With the use of sign language. Irene, encouraged viewers to love, and do God's will. Letting all people, see it was good to be a Christian, and to please Jesus.

It could be understood. That without a doubt. Irene's intention. Was to encourage others deaf persons. To love, and serve the Lord, as Christians:

> "Psalms 40:16 Let all those that seek thee rejoice and be glad in thee: **let such as love thy salvation say continually, The Lord be magnified.**"

> "Psalms 5:11 But **let all those that put their trust in thee rejoice:** let them ever shout for joy, because thou defendest them: **let them also that love thy name be joyful in thee.**"

Irene chose scripture verses. Which meant something special to her. And Irene spoke words on loving each other. She shared how from her observation. She knew Christian people, needed to love.

The one hand 'I love you' sign, was used by Irene, at the very end of Irene's sessions. It was a pleasure, for me to see Irene, revealing her delight in serving the Lord. It was a new lease on life as Irene became aware. People were with approval getting her messages.

Irene recognized she was doing God's will. And the Lord was fulfilling Irene's desire. To serve the Lord God by sharing God's word. It was a blessing for Irene, and myself.

Recording Message:

We went to Irene's residence. And did the video tapping of Irene's chosen message. Irene sharing the word of God. Was viewed by many. And still remains available for viewing:

"Psalms 143:6 **I stretch forth my hands unto thee**: my soul thirsteth after thee, as a thirsty land. Selah."

Irene's deaf friends also watched her videos. And at the start, gave as some disapproval. But Irene's, effort to serve God, was accepted.

Prayer Answered:

A shared, long time prayer for a job was answered. The time for the video-taping of Irene's TV ministry was gone. Yet another ministry opportunity presented itself, for Irene.

By going to Pastor Otis Brown's church. Irene, became involved in another way of offering herself. Irene's constant habit of reading. Led Irene to responded to the church bulletin's appeal. The church had a feeding ministry, and they asked for volunteers.

Irene answered the church-ad by the feeding ministry. And started serving. Serving the Lord by using herself weekly in the feeding ministry, was Irene's pleasure.

Irene, especially found delight in scrubbing the large pots used in providing meals. Another asset to Irene assisting in the church feeding ministry. Gave Irene God's assurance that she was in many ways pleasing.

Irene received expressions of gratitude, from individual church members for her work. Being of service to the Lord, using herself. Was also a fulfillment for Irene. As it turned out Irene soon was working a new job. And Irene, same as with the feeding ministry, handled large pots.

New Worship Opportunity:

Irene, being involved in a mid-week worship, service, involving deaf persons. Gave Irene, a much needed. And apparently, good change for Irene.

Bible study, with deaf peers, led Irene to attend a larger church. The church provided, a team of interpreters. And allowed Irene to have contact with many deaf, claiming they were, Christians.

Irene, at first was encouraged. And attended, many social events, with deaf Christians. The contact Irene had, assisted her Christian growth.

But unfortunately, at the large church. There were some, with effort, to make racial differences. And for that reason, Irene, stopped attending.

Growth Realized:

As Irene, continued to apply God's word. To her situations. Irene continued to trust the Lord. And Irene was blessed by knowing. In every situation, the Lord was with her. And the Lord was the one, she needed to know was satisfied with her.

From having occasional contact, with Irene. It became clear to me. Irene, wanted her life. To grow in pleasing the Lord. As a Deaf Christian witness for the Lord.

A Move That Blessed:

Irene moved, to her birth place, where she had a sister (also deaf). That allowed Irene to have closer, family contacts.

One of the most blessed, experiences Irene, shared. Was time with her two deaf sons, and her hearing daughter. Irene also was met for the first time.

Irene found a job where she moved, for which she was thankful. Irene soon found a church she was thankful for. The church, for which Irene was thankful. Was led by a good bible preaching minister, who is also deaf.

Many times, Irene e-mailed me. To share the message given by her deaf minister. Irene also shared, the scriptures, that were used. I, know the Lord, is blessing Irene:

> "John 12:26 **If any man serve me, let him follow me**; and where I am, there shall also my servant be: **if any man serve me, him will my Father honour.**"

CHAPTER 14

Lesson Learned

The number one thing I, am joyful about, from my, relationship with the Lord, God. I, am gaining knowledge, from experiencing, that the Lord is exactly as he says he is. And nothing ever changes God's love.

Whenever around me, there is any drama. I, know it is not from the Lord, that I, should be overcome, or stopped by it. I, know from experience. The Lord is well-able. To use all things for me, to abide in doing good.

Nothing in Christ Jesus is coincidental. Is another realization in my life. Nothing is unplanned by the Lord God. Even things, I did not care to experience, or see experienced by others. I, have learned. As I, go through, and in the dark, of the world.. The Lord God uses everything for good.

I, find it is in God's word, how God from history. Has proven, he works things for the good of his servants. When it comes to being exposed to attitudes, and adverse actions. I, stand in the name of the Lord.

I, learned because of my, will to serve Christ Jesus. Over the will of mankind. I, am in my journey constantly being prepared. Prepared for righteousness sake.

There is by the Lord God's grace. Nothing that I, face alone. And this is my joyful assurance, and confidence. I have the Lord's encouragement. And I, have found it is true, just as promised. The Lord, is always involved. In the inevitable, life events with me.

By abiding in Christ, and by knowing Christ abides in me. I, welcome the world's reaction towards me. I, learned I, need to face hostility for growth.

A very special blessing for me, is knowing. The Lord's promises are faithful, and true. The Lord's faithfulness is confirmed. In the fulfillment of the promises. The Lord sets before me.

I constantly seek to promote Christ's way. And I, rejoice in being encouraged by the Lord. Through, and in the dark. To look forward to Christ's, righteous kingdom:

> "**Blessed are they which are persecuted for righteousness' sake**: for theirs is the kingdom of heaven. Blessed are ye, when men shall revile you, and persecute you, and shall say all manner of evil against you falsely, for my sake. **Rejoice, and be exceeding glad: for great is your reward in heaven**: for so persecuted they the prophets which were before you. Matthew 5:10-12"

> "But **let all those that put their trust in thee rejoice**: let them **ever shout for joy**, because thou defendest them: let them also that love thy name **be joyful in thee**. Psalms 5:11"

"For his anger endureth but a moment; in his favour is life: weeping may endure for a night, but **joy cometh in the morning.** Psalm 30:5"

"Thou hast turned for me my mourning into dancing: **thou hast put off my sackcloth, and girded me with gladness;** To the end that **my glory may sing praise to thee**, and not be silent. O Lord my God, **I will give thanks unto thee for ever.** Psalm 30:11-12"

"Ye are **the light of the world**. A city that is set on an hill **cannot be hid.** Matthew 5:14"

"**Let your light so shine** before men, that they may see **your good works, and glorify** your Father which is in heaven. Matthew 5:16"

"Wherefore we receiving a kingdom which cannot be moved, **let us have grace, whereby we may serve God acceptably with reverence** and godly fear: For **our God is a consuming fire.** Hebrews 12:28-29"

OVERVIEW

"Through In The Dark", is basically the author's consideration of the experiences, which gave her growth in the Lord God. In adding to the Author's growth in trusting the Lord God (though darkness is present).

Shared are experiences, which promoted for the Author, soul security. And growing trust in who the Lord God says he is.

Very important to the Author is her need to share, the kind of worship the Lord God requires.

"Through And In The Dark", shares how the Lord revealed himself through the inspired TV ministries, produced by the Author, and her husband. And the blessings of connecting, and supporting others to share their efforts in serving the Lord.

How the Author after experiencing the false example of worship. Was relieved, to serve the Lord God his way. From struggles the Author learned to serve the Lord, without a struggle. The Author discloses, how worship hostility became a life revealing, and worship promoting blessing.

The Author shares ministry events, as that which was planned, and unplanned. In ministering to, and for the Lord God, the Author shares how the Lord, calls the shots, by presenting or removing perceived opportunities.

God's proven steadfast, love for the author, her husband, and other persons is also emphasized. Ministering for the Lord was seen as being completed by the Lord, in any role the Author had.

Identifying the Lord, in all activities (planned or unplanned), the Author fully identifies. The Lord God always ministers to his followers (In and through the dark).

The Lord God's presence ministering to the Author, is what the Author identifies. The Author discloses her treasure of recognizing she gives in ministry, only what she receives from the Lord.

The Author has confidently concluded, it is by the Lord God, ministering to mankind, which prepares his servants. All the Author needs for growth in her ability to minister, the Author recognizes, does not come from her effort.

All needed growth for ministry, is recognized by the Author, as coming from the Lord God. And although the Lord is seen as giving so much more than enough. For being able to know him.

To reveal who he is, and yet to know him to the utmost. We are left blessed, in and through the dark. The boxes mankind constructs holding their doctrines. Are altogether too small to hold all that the Lord God is. Which is the reason why, new birth takes more than becoming a believer!

"But will God in very deed dwell with men on the earth? behold, heaven and the heaven of heavens cannot contain thee; how much less this house which I have built!2 Chronicles 6:18"

"For now we see through a glass, darkly; but then face to face: now I know in part; but then shall I know even as also I am known. 1 Corinthians 13:12"

About the Author

From years of walking with the Lord God, the Author seeks to abide in service. Giving praise to the Lord God. The Author is totally sold out for her Creator. And the Author rejoices in the faithfulness, and leadership of her Lord. Who remains with her, in and through the dark.

CPSIA information can be obtained
at www.ICGtesting.com
Printed in the USA
BVHW031708280321
603591BV00005B/454